OLD WORLD CHARM

A WITCHES THREE COZY MYSTERY

CATE MARTIN

D1452710

CHAPTER 1

*L*ate December in the middle of a Minnesota snowstorm that couldn't decide between a whiteout of blowing flakes and icy sleet sharp enough to sting was no time to go down to a cellar. Especially if that cellar was like the one in Miss Zenobia Weekes' Charm School for Exceptional Young Ladies, which had just one way down, and that was from the backyard.

Luckily, being witches, we had ways of keeping a warm pocket of precipitation-free air around us as we went out the back door and around the protruding solarium to the cellar doors that were slanted just a few degrees above laying flat on the ground.

It might have felt like rubbing in my current lack of a wand when Brianna waved hers about before we were even down the steps to the cellar and the fire in the wood-burning stove flared to bright, crackling life.

It might have, but I knew Brianna didn't have a bone in her body capable of rubbing a thing in. She was only focused on creating more light and warmth.

But I still felt a little jab of sadness at my wandlessness. The warm bubble of dry air spell was never one Brianna had taught me, but making warmth and light had been one thing I had succeeded at.

Before my wand fell into the hands of an enemy witch. She had held it for just a moment, but that had been a moment too long. When I held my wand in my hands, it no longer felt like part of me. And I was pretty sure that it felt the same about me.

Brianna's shadow shrank and gained definition as she walked up to the wood-burning stove, then grew bigger and more diffuse as she continued past it, to another oven built into the stone wall itself.

She took the warm air bubble with her I realized as my back felt instantly cold. I turned to pull the cellar doors shut behind me just as the wind built up to a gust that whistled through the trees in shrieks and moans. The doors kept out the snow and sleet but not that ghostly howling.

I scurried down the wood steps to the stone floor, pulling my sweater closer around me despite the warmth of the fire I was approaching. It was still roaring and dancing over the logs, crackling and snapping as sap ignited. And the smoky smell of its cured wood burning cleanly went a long way to driving off the otherwise mildewy cellar smell. But the stones held on to the cold. Even through the soles of my winter boots I could feel the chill in the floor radiating up to my calves.

"I think we're ready," Brianna said from where she was peering into the oven built into the side of the fireplace. The fire had burned down to sullenly glowing embers, and compared to the wood-burning stove gave off almost no heat at all. "You should touch it."

"Yes, of course," I said. She stepped back, and I reached into the oven, past the charred remains of the logs we had placed within it the night before, and gingerly touched the metal box in the center.

It was cool, but not so chill as the stones under my feet. I grasped it more firmly then brought it out to set it on the closest workbench.

But I was reluctant to open it. "Is this the last thing we can try?" I asked.

"No, of course not," Brianna said. "There's always another thing to try."

"But if this doesn't work?"

"I'll have to branch out beyond the library here for that research," she said. "But don't worry about that now. Let's see if this worked. Because it really should have. I know you're worried, but I'm sure this is going to be okay."

I bit my lip but gave her a nod. I had told her all about my dreams, the ones that had plagued me since the night the witch Evanora had held my wand in her hands. Nightmares, really, about every possible thing that could go wrong while I had no wand to protect me. I was attacked in a million different ways, always reaching for a wand that wasn't there just before the latest nightmarish creature fell upon me and tore me to bits.

"They're just anxiety dreams," Brianna said, squeezing my hand. "And of course, you're anxious. That's completely understandable. The bond between a witch and a wand is a very special one."

I tried and failed at an answering smile, so I settled for another nod. Frankly, given how little magic my wand and I had ever managed to do together, Brianna was being beyond kind.

The clasp on the box wanted to stick, but I forced it open then threw back the lid. Inside was a bundle wrapped in cloth strips, like a very small, very elongated mummy. Brianna watched eagerly as I took out the bundle and carefully started unwinding the strips.

The cloth was not well made. Some of the threads were larger than others, and in some places the weave was so tight it bunched up while in others it was so loose it was beginning to unravel. But what can I say, it was my first attempt at weaving cloth.

Finally, I was down to the innermost wrappings, and I got my first glimpses of the wand within. It glistened in the firelight, still oily slick from the magical ointment I had rubbed into it the night before. Even after baking for a night and a day it wasn't quite dry yet.

This new ointment had brought out a golden tone in the blondish willow wood that hadn't been there before. It was actually quite pretty, but when I tipped my hand to admire the run of light up its length, I saw something else, something darker that slipped behind that flare of reflected light. I couldn't quite get my eyes to focus on it, but I knew I had seen something.

Then the wand was resting naked on my palm. It felt cool and slightly oily on my skin. I closed my hand around it, more an embrace than a squeeze. But it remained cold and inert. My flesh couldn't warm it. For the first time since before I had even worked it into a wand shape, it felt like I was holding just an ordinary stick.

"Nothing," I said with a sigh. "Nothing at all."

I put it back down on the mound of wrappings in the box then wiped my hand on my jeans. The oil remained, the minty but also sappy aroma clinging tenaciously to me.

"Maybe you should try a spell," Brianna said. "Just a small one. Something for both of you to remember each other. Like the light spell, you did to get those hoodlums to back off. Try that."

I looked down at the wand, rubbing the back of my hand against my lips and realizing too late I had somehow gotten ointment there as well. The taste was tarry, like a Scottish breakfast tea but stronger. It brought to mind a day from my childhood, a summer day so hot the pavement on the street was sticky. It had smelled a bit like this ointment tasted.

"Amanda?" Brianna said.

"Sorry," I said, picking up the wand again. "I'll give it a try."

I raised the wand then closed my eyes, summoning an image of what I wanted to create. I wasn't expecting anything as spectacular as what I had managed in the heat of a fight or flight moment. I only needed a few sparks.

I felt my own magical power flowing through me, but when it should have also flowed smoothly into my wand as an extension of my hand, it didn't.

It didn't stop entirely. But it did hesitate. Not like how the latch on the box had fought me, like something gone a bit rusty from disuse.

No, this felt like the wand was waiting for someone else's permission before accepting my power.

But it had accepted it. And now my power was flowing through the length of the wand. My eyes were still closed when the sparks began to appear, but I knew they were there. I could see the wand in my mind's eye, forming the little bursts of power as I had asked it to.

But it felt wrong. The wand wasn't part of me. It belonged to someone else. It was still willing to do my bidding, but only as long as it felt like it.

What if it was trying to lure me in, to get me to rely on it just so that in some moment of great need it could turn on me?

Suddenly the flow of energy felt less like something I was channeling through my wand and more like something the wand was pulling out of me. It was consuming that part of me, like a vampire.

I screamed and flung the wand away from me. Brianna threw up her arms and ducked as the bit of wood sailed in the space over her head and under the timbers of the low ceiling. Sparks trailed behind the flying wand in little clouds like exhaust from a jalopy in a cartoon.

Then it clattered to the stone floor and laid there, just an ordinary stick someone had sanded and polished to ridiculous perfection.

"That looked like it was working. What went wrong?" Brianna asked as she slowly straightened.

"I don't know. It's just not right," I said. "I see darkness in it, but never when I'm looking at it straight on. It feels like a cold, alien thing in my hand. And there's something choking the flow of energy between us. It's like there's someone else interfering between us somehow. I feel like it's just waiting to betray me."

Brianna chewed her lip for a moment then went to the workbench and retrieved the box and the wrappings. She used the cloth to pick up the wand without letting her skin touch it then laid it gently back in the box and snapped the lid shut.

Then she held the box out for me.

"What am I supposed to do with that?" I asked.

"I don't know," Brianna said. "But it's yours. Part of you. Your responsibility. I'll keep researching, but in the meantime, you have to do all you can to rebond with this wand. Keep it with you but try not to touch it. Just in case it really is trying to work against you."

I really wished she had just dismissed my impressions as silly. But she was taking me completely seriously. My stomach was knotting up even tighter than before.

I took the box and headed back up the stairs to the backyard, swinging open the door and stepping out into the storm. The wind caught my hair, coated it in sleet that froze on contact, then plastered it across my eyes. But I pressed on, crunching through layers of snow and ice until I was up the porch steps and into the solarium.

I had changed from boots to house slippers and was still trying to disentangle frozen hair from frozen eyelashes when Brianna finally joined me.

"You should have waited," she said, waving her wand over me. My hair was instantly dry, if just as chaotic as ever. Brianna didn't have Sophie's perfect hair skills, no more than I did. "I just had to grab a few things as long as I was down there."

"For what?" I asked as she kicked off her own snowy boots and pulled on a pair of knee-high red and green mukluk slippers.

"I want to check the labels on these bottles against what's listed in the book," she said, tapping the bulging pockets of her sweater. "It's possible the ointment we prepared wasn't quite right."

I doubted very much that Brianna had made any mistakes, but I didn't say so. She wouldn't be satisfied until she had double-checked all of her own work for herself.

"I'm starving," I said instead. "That soup must be ready by now, right?"

I'd been smelling it for most of the afternoon. Bits of beef browned to the height of umami, the sharpest of cheddar cheeses, dark beer and just a hint of cream. Mr. Trevor had been skeptical as he always was when he tried out a new recipe, but I was sure this beef and ale cheddar soup was going to be divine.

"Yeah, I think so," Brianna said absentmindedly. She was looking inside the pocket now, squinting at those labels. I wasn't sure how old the contents were, but the labels were written in a distinctly Victorian script.

"You're eating before you go upstairs," I said to her, grabbing her arm and pulling her into the kitchen when I saw she was indeed starting to go up the backstairs instead.

"But I just want to-"

"Food first," I said.

I'm not sure if it's because of all of the years I spent working in a diner or what, but when I'm upset, I always feel better when I can get someone else to eat something. It's weird. But I rolled with it, filling two bowls from the steaming, slow cooker and watching Brianna take several bites before giving in to my own growling stomach.

The first mouthful warmed me more than even Brianna's spell had done. Suddenly, as bad as things were with my traitor of a wand and my lack of other witchy skills, everything all felt manageable.

Or maybe it was just because it was New Year's Eve, when you swept out the old problems and welcomed in new opportunities.

"Hey girls," Sophie said from the doorway in an enticing drawl that immediately had my suspicions up. She was dressed in jeans and a sweater. The jeans as always looked crisply new, the dark blue color unfaded by washing, and her sweater lacked the stretched-out shape-less quality that most of mine shared.

Then I saw something flash in her hand. Something golden.

"What do you have there?" I asked.

"Funny you should ask," she said, sliding into an empty seat at the table. She was holding whatever it was close to her chest and covering it with her hands, but then with a flourish, she slapped it down into the middle of the table.

"What is it?" Brianna asked as if just noticing she was there.

"An invitation," Sophie said. "A party invitation. It's just what we need right?"

"What sort of party?" Brianna asked.

"What sort of party? Don't you know what night this is?"

"New Year's Eve," I said, and Brianna nodded. "But why would someone do up formal invitations like this and then not deliver them until hours before? Most people make their plans way ahead of time."

Although not us, apparently.

"We've been a little lax in checking the mail," Sophie said.

"Mr. Trevor does that," Brianna said.

"He does here, yes," Sophie said. When she saw neither of us were following her, she added, "here and now."

"Oh," Brianna said as I pulled the card closer to get a proper look at it. Then I turned it over and saw a handwritten note on the back. This script was pretty far from the formal Victorian handwriting on the bottles in Brianna's pocket. This was the handwriting of a girl who was being subjected to the finest of educations but was doing her best not to let a bit of it sink in.

"Coco," I said.

"Coco is having a party?" Brianna asked.

"Coco's parents," I said, showing her the front of the card.

"Oh," she said, then more slowly as the significance of that dawned on her, "Oh. A 1927 party."

"Soon to be 1928," Sophie said with a wide grin.

"Ooh, we have to go," Brianna said, clapping her hands together with glee. I had never seen Brianna get that excited about anything that wasn't an ancient text written in a forgotten language.

"It's just what we need," Sophie said. "A 1920s party. It'll be divine. I'm sure the weather there is nicer than it is here."

"It has to be," Brianna said.

They were both so excited they were glowing. It almost hurt to look directly at them.

I looked down at the card in my hands.

To my shame, my first thought was not of Evanora and whether this was a trap. Sure, that was my second thought, and the one I couldn't shove aside.

But my first thought was of Edward, and whether he was also going to be at this party. My brain was certain that would be a bad idea since we had decided to take a big step back from all relationships and focus on the being a witch thing. But my heart was oblivious to what my brain was dictating. It just kept knocking hard against my ribs.

"Amanda, don't you agree?" Sophie asked.

"This is perfect, Amanda," Brianna said. "It will take your mind off of your wand problem."

"Oh, right," Sophie said. "How did that go?"

Brianna gave her a short shake of her head.

"I'm not sure this is wise," I said. "What if Evanora is there?"

"At the party?" Sophie asked.

"Anywhere near the party," I said. "She could be watching the school, waiting for us to cross the time bridge. Even if the party itself isn't a trap, she might be laying one of her own."

"We'll be careful," Sophie said.

"Search spells," Brianna said. "We can keep an eye out for her. And you won't be alone this time. We'll be with you."

"She might not be alone anymore either," I said. I had taken some of the edge off of their enthusiasm. I felt like the worst sort of killjoy. I might not have earned a break, but they both could use one.

"If you really want to go, we'll go," I said, and Brianna started hopping up and down in her chair, hands clapping again. "But we have to be careful. Really, really careful."

"We will," Sophie promised, squeezing my hand. "To be honest, I kind of want to go back to the past and lure this witch out for what she did to you. But not tonight. Tonight, we party."

I sighed, but then forced a smile on my face. "All right. Tonight, we party."

CHAPTER 2

*N*ew Year's Eve 1927 in St. Paul was cold. Deadly cold. But at least the sky was clear, there was no wind, and while there was snow on the ground, none of it was blowing down from the sky.

I could live with that.

"Let's get inside the school first," I said, hustling Sophie and Brianna up the back steps as quickly as I could given the fact that the steps were icy and we were all wearing party shoes and not our usual winter boots.

"Why?" Sophie asked.

"We said we'd be careful," I said. "We need to take a look around before we go to that party, and I'd rather do that indoors."

"Good idea," Brianna said. We went through the solarium and past the kitchen to the dining room, mainly because the bay window there had a view of the house next door, all lit up for the party. Not that I was going to use my eyes for the looking around, but facing the right direction felt appropriate.

"I know some detecting spells, but Sophie has more raw ability with sensing other magic," Brianna said.

"And you have that thing you do," Sophie added.

"We should each do what we know and compare notes after," I said.

"I'll be in the library," Brianna said, her wool coat flapping behind her as she raced for the stairs.

"I'll take the parlor," Sophie said.

"I don't need to be alone," I said.

"We might, actually," Sophie said. "We've not all tried to do this sort of thing before. We don't know what can happen if we overlap or anything. Better safe than sorry, right?"

I couldn't argue with that. I pulled out the chair where Mr. Trevor always sat and turned it towards the window then sat down. Night was darker here than in 2018, and from the height of the chair, the branches of the tree outside the window blocked the light from the house next door. All I could see now was my own reflection.

I liked the dress. I'll confess that. I really liked the dress. Sapphire blue with an art deco pattern worked in it with silver thread. It was crazy gorgeous.

Not to mention my hair. Normally I had a love/hate relationship with my hair, and we agreed to coexist without troubling each other too much. But Sophie had brushed it out then twisted it up, stuck a few pins in it, and added a peacock feather to match my dress. She spent maybe five minutes on it but when she was done it was perfect. My chaos of curls were now arranged in neat rows that were very 1927 appropriate.

It was magic.

Somehow, in the process of dressing and letting Sophie do my hair, I had found myself getting actually excited about this party. I had to take a few breaths and focus before that died down and I could turn my mind to the task at hand.

I had my wand with me, buried inside the beaded bag which matched my dress, but I didn't need it for what I was about to do. I had done it before I had ever bonded with my wand. I'd be fine.

I took another deep breath then closed my eyes. Then my awareness opened in that other world, the world where I could see the threads that formed all things.

It might have been better to try this in the yard. All of the magic that infused the very walls of Miss Zenobia's school really skewed what I was seeing. But it was too cold out there, and I knew how to move my awareness around.

I drew out the threads that would connect my current form with my temporarily inert body and keep it breathing while I was out of it, then I passed through the walls and out into the yard between the two houses.

The house was already full of people, but no one appeared out of the ordinary. I expanded my awareness further, sensing the entire neighborhood, but there was no sign of another magical being. It was possible that Evanora was having the house watched by a non-witch – I knew she worked with gangsters and tricked them into doing her bidding – but I was willing to risk it.

I opened my eyes and found Sophie and Brianna leaning against the wall on either side of the bay window. They straightened as I blinked.

"All good?" I asked.

"I'm only getting the usual feelings of a large group of people gathered together," Sophie said. "Some of them have tensions with each other, but they seem like they'll set them aside for the night. Definitely no one magical."

"I didn't detect any magic person, object, or remnant of a spell," Brianna said. "I was very thorough."

"It looks good to me too," I said, getting up from the chair. "Shall we?"

We headed out towards the front door. The hooks for coats that were largely empty in our time were overburdened with coats, scarves, and mittens on strings here.

"Our predecessors are having a night in, it seems," Sophie said.

"Yeah," I said, but felt a shiver run up my spine as I remembered that although we could see no one, they were all still there. At this very minute, my body could be overlapping with one of theirs. We might be existing in the very same space, if only for a moment. It was an uncomfortable feeling.

"I just thought," Sophie said, her hand on the door but not opening it. "We know that house burns down at some point, right? Before there are condos."

"Those condos were built in the 1970s," I said.

"But there was another house inbetween," Sophie said.

"It's all right," Brianna said, but her cheeks were flushing. Sophie and I kept watching her until she spoke again. "I looked it up. This house doesn't burn down until 1939. So it's quite safe for now."

I wished I found that more reassuring. Lots of things could still go wrong short of burning the whole house down.

Sophie was looking at me with her eyebrows raised in question, and I gave her a nod. She swung the door open, and we bustled back out into the cold, holding onto each other as we went down the icy steps and along the front walk then up the sidewalk to the house next door.

It was barely nine, but when the front door opened, we saw the hallway beyond stuffed with people. They milled about in groups on the parquet floor of the hall as well as against the railings of the over-looking balconies on the second and third floors and even on the stairs. They were holding punch or wine glasses and little plates of food, laughing together in a joyous cacophony. Most of the men were wearing top hats and fancy suits, and while most of the women were dressed too conservatively to be called flappers, they still had gowns of dazzling colors with plenty of jewelry and usually some bit of frippery tying back their hair.

"Awesome," Sophie said after the servant who had answered the door had glanced at our invitation then waved us passed.

Heads turned as Sophie moved through the hall. Her dress was far from conservative, a deep red with sequins that caught the light, the skirt short with a beaded hem that clattered as she walked. Her sequined headband was adorned with a red feather that curled around her ear. I was a little nervous that someone would say something rude to her. The only other people of color I could see were either serving food or playing in the band I could just glimpse through the open doors to the ballroom. But if Sophie ever felt nervous, she didn't let it show. And all the looks she was drawing were either admiring or frankly envious.

"Should we try the food first?" Brianna asked as she and I trailed in Sophie's wake. Her gown was more like mine, not as attention-grabbing as Sophie's number, but its deep emerald color looked lovely with her long red hair spilling around her shoulders.

"We should find Coco, I think," I said, although in truth it wasn't her I was scanning the crowd in search of. "To thank her for the invitation."

"Maybe she's by the buffet," Brianna said hopefully.

I laughed. "All right, we'll start there. Those deviled eggs do look tempting."

"And look at all that cheese!" Brianna said.

A wave of applause rolled through the ballroom as the band struck up an apparently popular number. I didn't recognize it, but it had the sort of rhythm you could dance the Charleston to. Couples started peeling away from the line, spinning to join the others already dancing.

"Champagne?" Sophie offered as she appeared from nowhere with a glass for each of us.

"Thanks," I said, taking a sip. The bubbles promptly went up my nose, nearly making me sneeze.

"I took a spin around the hall, but I don't see Edward," Sophie said.

"Edward? I thought we were looking for Coco," Brianna said.

"We are," I said.

"I didn't see her either, but she's pretty young for this crowd," Sophie said. "Maybe we should check her room?"

"I hope her parents approved of her inviting us," Brianna said. "I hadn't even thought that we might be crashers."

"It's a big party. No one is going to question us being here," Sophie said.

"Have you ever been in this house before?" Brianna asked. "Do you know where her room is?"

"I've not been in here physically," I said. "I have sort of cast my mind through it. I would think her room is on one of the upper floors, probably out of bounds for partygoers."

"She invited us; I'm sure she'll come looking for us," Sophie said, sipping at a glass of champagne I hadn't even see her acquire.

And indeed, by the time we had plates of food and had found a spot at one of the tall tables around the periphery of the room Coco had found us. She raced across the room, narrowly avoiding several dancing couples. Another older girl was trailing behind her, scowling at everything around her.

Although they were nearly the same height, Coco was still dressed like a child while the other girl was wearing a grown-up gown and I realized that despite the baby fat she was the older of the two. Coco was all bright and sparkly with a beaded headband holding her thick hair back from her face. The other girl was the very opposite, wearing a gown that would not have been an eye-catching color even before it had grown faded with time. Her dull brown hair was pulled back in a severe updo that looked painfully tight. And her round face was strangely colorless. Not just pale or ivory-like most of the winter skin on display around us, but outright colorless.

"I'm so glad you came!" Coco cried. "Do you like my dress?" She gave a little spin so we could see how the pink skirt moved around her.

"It's lovely," Sophie said. Coco beamed, but the girl who had walked up to us with her seemed to if anything scowl more deeply.

"Who's your friend?" I asked.

"Oh, this is Charlotte," Coco said, then her cheeks flushed a deep crimson. She drew her back of straighter and clasped her hands together. "I mean, may I present Charlotte Taylor? Charlotte, this is Amanda, Brianna, and Sophie. I'm sorry; I don't know your family names."

"Amanda Clarke," I said, wiping my hand on a napkin before extending it to the sullen girl. "Your dress is lovely. I love that shade of green. It's like the first buds in spring, isn't it?"

"It's my sister's dress," Charlotte said, but her sullenness did lighten up just a degree.

"Charlotte's sister is my sister Ivy's best friend since forever," Coco said. "They're the same age, though. Charlotte and I don't even go to the same school."

"Coco, we came down here to get some food," Charlotte said.

"In a minute," Coco said.

"I'm hungry," Charlotte persisted.

Coco sighed but took a deep breath and forced a smile. "Go get in line. I'll be right with you." She kept that tight smile focused on Charlotte until she finally turned and walked to the end of the line at the buffet.

"You're in charge of entertaining her, I'm guessing," I said.

"Yes," Coco sighed. "She doesn't like any of the same things I do. I don't think she really likes anything at all. Not anymore. She used to be nicer when we were younger. I mean, not a lot, but I could at least talk to her then."

"Aren't you still a little young for this sort of party?" Sophie asked her, taking another sip from her champagne as if to underscore that fact.

"Oh, yes," Coco said, all but bouncing with excitement. "Normally I'd be staying at my grandparents' house when my parents host a party like this, but this time I'm allowed."

"You're not fourteen yet?" Sophie asked.

"No, but almost," Coco said. "No, it's just that this is a special occasion, and my parents wanted the whole family here."

"You mean the party isn't just a New Year's Eve party?" I asked.

"No. The invitations didn't mention it, but my sister Ivy is going to make a big announcement this evening," Coco said. Then she waved for us to bring our heads closer to hers. Not that she could whisper anything to us and be heard over the band and the noise from the crowd, but she did lower it as much as she could. "Just between us, it's not going to be what everyone is expecting. I can't tell you what I know since I promised to keep it secret, but this party is going to be very exciting indeed. Some people here are going to be, and I'm not exaggerating, quite shocked."

"Is that what Charlotte is upset about?" Sophie asked. "Does she know this secret too?"

"No," Coco said with a dismissive wave. "I mean, yes, she does. She was there the same time as I was, with her sister, when Ivy told us. But that's not why she's acting almost rude. She's been like that all day."

"She's trying to get your attention," Brianna said, and we all turned to look at Charlotte nearly at the head of the line waving for Coco to join her.

"I better go," Coco said. "We're not supposed to be down here for more than getting food, but I wanted to say hello to you."

"And we wanted to thank you for the invitation," I said. "This party is amazing."

"You're welcome!" Coco said, beaming at us. Then that conspiratorial twinkle was back in her eye. "Be sure to enjoy yourselves as much as you can before the big announcement. The mood of this party is definitely going to shift after that."

She backed away so she could keep looking at us with that hinting gleam to her eyes.

"What was that all about?" Brianna asked when Coco was quite gone.

"The big announcement has to be an engagement, right?" Sophie said. "We know Ivy was playing the market. I guess she's made her choice."

"And not a conventional one, to judge by Coco's little hints," Brianna said.

They both looked to me, but my attention was focused on the last of the cheese crumbs left on my plate.

I knew what they were both thinking. I was thinking it too. For a family as wealthy as Ivy and Coco's, the shocking choice would be to marry someone not wealthy.

And that meant Edward.

"Do you want to go?" Sophie asked.

"Maybe we should go," Brianna said. I looked up at both of them. Despite how badly they had both wanted to come to this party, there

18

was none of that longing in their eyes now. They weren't just being polite. They would genuinely leave with me if I didn't want to stay.

"No, I'm okay," I said. "Edward was never..."

But I couldn't quite find the word for what Edward never was. And they were both still looking at me with so much concern it made my heart ache. I had never had friends that felt so much like sisters.

"I'm okay," I said, and my voice didn't warble this time. "This was always going to happen, right? We're decades in the past. It already has happened. I'm okay."

"Then we should dance," Sophie said, setting down her champagne glass to take Brianna and me by the hand and pull us out on the dance floor.

CHAPTER 3

*I*t quickly became apparent that letting Sophie drag me out onto the dance floor had been a very bad idea. I had no idea how to dance the Charleston. I'm pretty challenged with not looking like a spaz when dancing to modern music. And it clearly was not yet a thing for three young women to form a circle and dance for each other rather than waiting for a man to come along.

We got a lot of stares. Some of the young women standing close to the wall in groups were tittering at us. Not kindly. I went to high school. I know what it sounds like when the mean girls are laughing at you.

But Sophie was oblivious to it all. She had left behind her lifelong ambition to be a ballet dancer when the three of us were called to take on the guardianship of Miss Zenobia Weekes' Charm School for Exceptional Young Ladies. I had never actually seen her dance ballet, only the sort of dancing she did that channeled her magic.

What she was doing now wasn't like either of them. She seemed to draw in what the other dancers around us were doing and worked the bits she liked into a tapestry of movement that was still largely driven by her own interpretation of the music. She was having a ball.

Then the band started playing for her, improvising extra bits to see what she would do with them. And she was wonderful. But with every spin and backbend she worked into her dance, more eyes were on us.

I tripped on the end of my gown and took that as an irrefutable sign, stumbling off the dance floor to collapse against the wall and catch my breath. I tried to see if I had torn the back of my gown when it had caught on the heel of my shoe. It would be a shame to destroy something so lovely, even if I had no idea when I would ever wear it again.

A roar echoed through the room, and a few people broke into spontaneous applause as Sophie danced her way down to a split that somehow her skirt accommodated, then burst up like a red-beaded rocket high into the air.

I realized to my surprise that Brianna was still out there, dancing away. She was no more coordinated than I was, but she didn't seem to mind a bit what she looked like or what those young women watching her were thinking. She just had her eyes closed, moving her arms and legs in whatever manner she wished.

I wish I could do that. Just tune the rest of the world out and be myself. But then, Brianna being herself is sort of apart from the rest of the world just by her very nature.

I had never thought about that before. I knew that Sophie had left someone behind when she'd left New Orleans. She never told us his name or anything about him, but I knew he existed. And I had left an adopted family behind when I came to the charm school but had quickly found friendships with two guys in two different time periods. I just always made connections with people. But Brianna didn't seem like she ever did. She had an old mentor that she spoke with, but I'm not sure how close their bond was.

Was Brianna lonely? She didn't seem unhappy. But maybe there was more Sophie and I could be doing to draw her out.

Like this party. This had been a good idea. Even if the other people in the house with us seemed largely superfluous to Brianna.

I turned my attention back to my skirt, but as much as I twisted, I couldn't get a clear view of where I thought I might have ripped it.

"Oh dear," said one of the young women. I bristled, steeling myself for a mock show of concern that was really going to contain a dozen barbs about how I didn't fit in. But this young woman was standing apart from the others, setting aside a glass of champagne that looked untouched as her hands reached out to me.

She sounded sincere. The concern in her large blue eyes felt sincere. But there was something about the shade of her brown hair, the structure of her face. It was reminding me of someone I didn't trust. But who?

I flinched as her hands closed on my arm, but she was just turning me a bit so she could see the back of my dress. She made a tisking sound. "Come with me. I can fix that in a jiffy," she said, linking her arm through mine and leading me out of the ballroom. I tried to catch either Brianna or Sophie's eyes, but they were both too caught up in the dancing to see me being dragged away.

Was this one of Evanora's witches? Was I being led into a trap?

"Do I know you?" I asked, but she didn't answer as she led me down a short corridor to a softly lit room. By day I'm sure it was the lady of the house's parlor, with over-stuffed chairs close to the fireplace and tables perfectly positioned for serving tea. The young woman let go of my arm and started digging through the drawers in a desk under a window that looked out on the back garden. Torches had been placed around the edges of the patio that had been swept clear of snow.

"Here we go," she said, turning back to me with one hand closed around something I couldn't see and a pair of sharp scissors in the other. The light from the fire raced down the length of the scissors as she turned.

"Who are you?" I asked again, trying not to sound panicked. I clutched my bag, felt the shape of my wand within. Not that it would help me.

"Oh, I'm sorry," she said, lowering the scissors to a less aggressive position. "You asked before. I was distracted trying to remember were Ivy's mother kept her sewing kit. Not that she sews, but this room is always the emergency retreat for us ladies when there are parties on." She seemed to realize she was rambling without quite answering the question and blushed, then switched the scissors to her other hand so she could offer the empty one to shake. "Mary Taylor."

"Mary Taylor," I said, still trying to figure out why she seemed sort of familiar. But then it clicked. Her hair, her face, even the color of her eyes, was the same as Charlotte's. But her temperament softened the features that seemed too harsh in her little sister. "You're Charlotte's sister."

"Yes! Yes, I am," Mary said.

"I'm Amanda Clarke," I said, finally shaking her hand. "I'm a friend of Coco's."

"Coco is such a vivacious girl," Mary said.

"Yes, she is."

"Come," Mary said, taking my arm again and bringing me closer to the fireplace. "Can you turn a bit? I need more light."

"For what?" I asked. While Mary had none of Charlotte's glowering negativity, I still wasn't sure I wanted to turn my back to her and those scissors.

"You have a tear in your skirt. But don't worry! I have a very good hand. I'll stitch it up in a jiffy, and no one will ever be able to tell the difference," she said.

"Oh, that's very kind of you," I said.

"I'm sure you would do the same for me if our roles were reversed," Mary said, squatting low to examine the tear at the hem of my dress then fishing a needle and a spool of thread out of the little sewing kit.

"I might like to, but believe me, if I did it, everyone would see the seam," I said. Mary laughed.

"My mother was a seamstress. I used to help her sometimes. This is a pretty simple mend, really. I can see that your heel caught here from the scuff on the inside of the skirt, but it pulled over here right at the seam. That's easy to hide the mending," Mary said, her eyes focused on threading the needle. She did it in one go then set to work.

"Coco tells me this party is going to end with a surprise," I said. "Do you have any idea what she's talking about?"

"Ivy's parents are announcing her engagement," Mary said. "But that's not exactly a surprise."

"She's been holding court for a while, to hear Coco tell it," I said.

Mary laughed. "That's quite a way to put it. Yes, I suppose she has, but truly her heart has always been settled on just one man."

"Coco said you two were best friends," I said. "You and Ivy."

"Since we were too young to talk," Mary said and smiled up at me. "It's a shame Coco and Charlotte were so far apart in age, or they could be friends too."

"I'm not sure even then they would have much in common," I said.

"That's true," Mary said. "Coco is very unique. Her parents are going to have their hands full when she comes of age."

"Oh, I don't think she'll be running with boys," I said.

"Nor I," Mary said, snipping the end of the thread then taking my extended hand to pull herself back up onto her feet. "Unless those boys are pirates, or rumrunners, or perhaps even revolutionaries."

Now it was my turn to laugh. "That does sound just like Coco."

Mary was smiling back at me, but then the smile melted away into a look of confusion. "She exaggerates and tells stories, but never outright lies. I wonder what she means that Ivy has some surprise in store? She's never said anything like that to me."

"I thought perhaps her choice of fiancé might be a touch scandalous," I said.

Mary's frown deepened. "Because he's poor or because he was raised in an orphanage, you mean?"

"I'm not judging," I said. "I just thought that might be the shock Coco meant."

"No, it can't be that," Mary said. "Everyone knows how much Ivy adores Edward. You only have to spend a moment or two with them when they're in a room together to feel that."

I bit at my lip and tried to keep an interested look on my face, but in truth, those words stabbed a little. I had never met Ivy or seen the two of them together, but I had heard Edward talk of Ivy. I had known how much he thought of her since the moment I first met him. But clearly, I hadn't let myself give any thought to Ivy's end of things.

"Her parents?" I prompted.

"Love him," Mary said earnestly. "Ivy's father is full of praise for his intelligence and work ethic. With his good character, there is no limit to how far he'll go. That's what he says, and I know Ivy's mother adores him. And just between us, I think his lack of living family is a plus for her. Now she doesn't have to share Ivy with another prominent family. In all but name, she'll still be a McTavet."

"It sounds like they'll be very happy together," I said.

"I hope so," Mary said, turning to put the sewing kit away. "Ivy has always been very good to me. After my father died and left us penniless, most of my friends from school just disappeared. But not Ivy."

"It's so strange for me to be here," I said. "Do you know I've never even met Ivy? Only Coco."

"And how do you know Coco?" Mary asked, once more linking her arm in mine as we walked back to the ballroom.

"She's helped me with a few things since I came to town in October," I said. "I live just next door."

"You're from the charm school?" Mary asked, and her eyes got even wider than usual.

"Yes."

"I'm sorry I didn't place your name before, but Coco has told me so many things about you and your friends," Mary said.

"What sorts of things?" I asked.

"Well, one does have to take Coco's stories with a grain of salt," Mary said, which pretty much answered my question. Coco hadn't seen any of us do anything magical, but she *had* helped us solve a murder. That was story enough. "And you know Edward?" Mary said, looking not at me but at the open doors to the ballroom.

"I do," I said. I really didn't want to say more than that.

"And Edward's friends," Mary went on.

"Some of them," I admitted. "Why?"

"Because that alarming gentleman has been watching us since we came out of the parlor, and I'm fairly certain it's not me he's looking to talk to," Mary said.

I looked up to see a solitary figure leaning against the doorframe at one of the few places where the light from the ballroom didn't fall. While most of the men around us were in top hats and tails, black and white like the penguins they are often shown as in cartoons, he was wearing a suit of bottle green, the coat long but without tails. His thumbs were resting in the pockets of a dark violet waistcoat, the golden chain of a pocket watch spanning between them.

Mary, still clutching my arm, came to an abrupt halt as the man pushed away from the doorframe to walk towards us. Then he pushed back his bottle-green bowler hat, and I saw his eyes.

"Hello, Amanda," he said.

"Hello, Otto," I replied.

CHAPTER 4

Otto was grinning at me, waiting for Mary to leave before speaking. But Mary recoiled against me, reading that grin as more of a leer. She clutched my arm tightly.

"It's okay, Mary," I said, putting my hand on hers until she relaxed her grip.

"You know him?" Mary asked.

"Yes. Like you said, he's a friend of Edward's," I said. Otto's grin ticked up a notch at that.

But the look of concern on Mary's face didn't diminish. She leaned close to whisper in my ear. "That's not all he is."

"I know," I said. "I'll be all right. Perfectly safe. I was actually hoping to run into him, although I had no idea he would be here at this party."

"Yes," Mary said, giving him a side eye. She hadn't expected to see him at the party either, although how much she really knew about him, I had no idea.

"Go on ahead," I said, giving her a little nudge towards the ball-room. "Get me a glass of champagne. I'll be there in just a minute."

Mary nodded, then reached up and touched my head. I almost flinched away, but she was just adjusting something in my hair. Then she smiled, dropped the smile to give Otto a minimally polite curt nod, then slipped through a gaggle of partygoers lingering in the doorway to disappear in the ballroom.

"What did you ever do to her?" I asked Otto.

"Her? Nothing," Otto said. "I guess she doesn't like my outfit."

"You don't really fit in here," I said.

"Wouldn't want to," Otto said with a dismissive snort.

"I'm guessing you're here for Edward," I said. His eyes searched my face, but I knew I had kept my voice perfectly neutral when I had said Edward's name.

"I am," he said. "But I'm not the only member of my profession in attendance."

"Really," I said, looking around at the men around us with new eyes. "They all look perfectly ordinary to me."

"Camouflage," Otto said.

"And you're more of a peacock," I said.

"I am who I am," he shrugged. Then he took my elbow and pulled me a little further from the light spilling from the doorway, into the shadows. I was getting a little annoyed with people leading me around, but his eyes were deadly serious when he turned to face me.

"What is it?" I asked, clutching my bag again. My bag, and the useless wand inside.

"You told her you were hoping to run into me," he said.

"I was just putting her at ease," I said.

"Just?"

"Well, also," I said, and then I was the one moving further away from the sounds of the party. Otto gamely followed. "Evanora. I'm guessing you haven't had any run-ins with her?"

"Not I," Otto said.

"Then others?"

Otto shrugged. "I hear rumors. She definitely is moving through the same circles as I do. I think she's been avoiding me. But..."

"But?" I said when his words trailed off.

He sighed. "I might be being paranoid. Probably am. Lots of things are up in the air now since Dapper Dan was murdered."

"Dapper Dan was murdered?" I said. "That was the guy you

mentioned before, the one who enforces the rules between cops and gangsters, right?"

"He was," Otto said. "Until someone put a bomb in his car."

"You have car bombs in 1927?"

His eyebrows knit together, and I remembered that as much as he knew I traveled through time, I should be more careful to keep my voice down.

"It's the first I've heard of someone bombing a car," he said. "You get a lot of that in the future?"

"Never mind. I shouldn't have said anything. Tell me why you think you're paranoid. Or rather, why you might not be paranoid."

"I feel like I'm being watched," Otto said.

"By the police or by other gangsters?" I asked.

"Either? Both? I don't know," he said, taking off his hat to run a hand through his hair. "Maybe neither. Because it's always women. Every time I get that itchy 'someone is spying on me' feeling and I look around, all I see are women."

"Women, more than one?"

"Not at the same time," Otto said. "But never the same one twice."

"How many times?" I asked.

"That I've noticed?"

"Obviously."

"Twelve."

"Twelve and then it stopped?"

"Exactly," Otto said. I didn't know if the number meant anything to him, though. But twelve plus Evanora made thirteen.

"Twelve precisely?" I asked. "That exact number?"

"Yes, woman," Otto said. "Do I seem like a person with a poor grasp of details to you?"

"No, but it's important to be clear," I said.

"What does it mean?" he asked.

"I don't know," I said. "You don't see any of them here, do you?"

"No," he said. "I've been making the rounds through the whole party. Lots of enemies here, but a lot of my own boys as well. And a few who are the worst sort, trying to play for both teams at once. But no sign of any of those women."

"Did you get the sense they wanted you to see them?" I asked.

Otto half-closed his eyes as he consulted his memory. "I hadn't thought of that. Maybe they did. They were subtle about it, though."

"None of that hazy memory thing that Evanora does?" I asked.

"No, I can picture them all in my head clear as day. If they do come here, I'll spot them."

"They aren't here," I said. "Brianna, Sophie and I were sure of that before we came inside. But I should tell them what's going on, just in case."

"What *is* going on?" Otto asked.

"I don't know," I admitted. "Except it sounds like Evanora is not the only witch roaming the dark corners of 1927."

"Soon to be 1928," Otto said. "Let's go in the ballroom. I could use a drink."

"So are you here because it's a gangster-friendly party, or because of the big announcement?" I asked as we strolled back towards the light and the music.

"Oh, you know about that, do you?" Otto asked.

"It seems to be all anyone is talking about," I said.

"Indeed," Otto said. The word had a gritty quality as if he were speaking with his jaw clenched tightly.

"I'm surprised to find you here, actually. I didn't get the sense that you approved," I said.

"Of Edward marrying Ivy?" Otto asked. "No, not remotely. But he's like a brother to me. I would never turn my back on him."

A waiter passed by with a tray, and Otto deftly caught two of the champagne glasses without even detaining the man. He handed one to me, and I took a sip.

"And you're here as well," Otto said, drinking his entire glass in one swallow.

"I didn't know about the announcement," I said. "Sophie and Brianna just thought a New Year's Eve party would be a nice break from our usual grind."

"Grind?"

"I mean work," I said.

"I got that," Otto said. "I'm just not sure what you consider work." Then a dark look passed over his eyes. "I'm not sure I want to consider it."

"It's mostly not like what you saw before," I said. The warmth in my cheeks was only partially from the champagne. Mostly it was shame at the memory of the last time the two of us had been together. Our lives had been in danger, but the dark power I had channeled still frightened me. "I don't usually do… that."

"Hey," Otto said, glancing around us then leaning closer to me. "I'm not judging you. As far as I'm concerned, you saved my life. Whatever you did, or however you did it, and whatever price you had to pay, I'm grateful."

"One could argue you were only in danger because of me in the first place," I said.

"One might. I won't," Otto said, then snatched another glass of champagne from a passing waiter. This one he took a mere sip from. "So you didn't know about the surprise part of the evening's festivities when you got here." I shook my head. "But after you found out, you stayed?"

"I'm all right," I said. He gave me a skeptical look. "I am. I already told you…" But this time I couldn't keep my voice neutral. It was catching and not letting go. And it wasn't about Edward. Or it wasn't just about Edward. I swallowed then forced words out past the thickening of my throat. "You remember what I said."

"I do," Otto said, once more standing almost too close beside me, eyes moving all around us to make sure no one was close enough to overhear. "And I know why you said it. You have something inside of you most people don't have, and it scares you. And you want to protect Edward from that. I get it."

"Also the time thing," I said.

"Whatever, it doesn't matter," Otto said.

"It does," I said.

"It's why you think that you and Edward don't belong together," he said. "But it doesn't change what's in your heart, does it? And you're going to stand here and watch him pledge himself to another? And that isn't going to crush you?"

I looked down at the champagne still fizzing in my glass and blinked hard. I kept blinking, over and over, until the danger of tears was passed.

"You're not just here for Edward, are you?" I asked.

"Well, I didn't know you'd be here," he said. He was about to say more when the song the band was playing ended and the ballroom reverberated with applause.

There was another sound buried beneath all the clapping and hooting and laughter, one that only slowly became clearer as people fell silent. A metallic ringing like a chime or a bell, coming from the front hall.

Then the butler appeared in the doorway and spoke with the voice of a Shakespearean actor, filling the room without the need for shouting. "Mr. and Mrs. McTavet are about to make an announcement. Ladies and gentlemen, if you'll just step this way."

No one seemed surprised by this. They just gathered in pairs, linked arms and strolled out of the ballroom and out onto the parquet floor of the main hall.

"Do you want to run away?" Otto asked me.

"A little," I admitted.

"I have my car just across the street," he said, and I could see he was serious.

"Running away isn't going to change anything, though, is it?"

"No, but a tragedy is still a tragedy with or without witnesses."

"We're Edward's friends," I said. "We should be here for him, especially as he has no family to stand with him. We can't leave. And stop calling it a tragedy."

"As you wish," he said, then held out his arm to me. "Shall we?"

I hesitated. I still really, really wanted to run away. I wasn't even sure that Edward would want me there. He hadn't invited me, probably didn't even know that Coco had. Would it be awkward? Would my presence ruin his happy day?

No, I told myself and slipped my arm through Otto's. I wasn't going to ruin anything. If it looked like my being there was weird, I would simply disappear. But if Edward was about to be engaged to another, I wanted to be there, to show that I was all right.

Not that I thought he thought I wouldn't be. Ugh, feelings are so confusing.

"Shall we?" Otto asked.

"Yes," I said, and the two of us together made our way into the hall-way, prepared to feign happiness to whatever degree was required.

For Edward.

CHAPTER 5

*A*t first glance, the hall looked far too crowded for us to get into. Everyone's heads were tilted back, looking towards the top of the stairs. I guessed that was where the chiming sound was coming from. But I couldn't see what everyone was looking at, and all of the men in their top hats weren't helping.

But I quickly found that crowds tended to part to let Otto through. He didn't say anything, and no one seemed to be looking his way, but there was always a gap in front of him that he could slip through. We made it through the mass of people milling about in the ballroom doorway to a spot against the wall, but at least from here; I could see all of the way up the staircase.

A man I took to be Ivy's father was standing on the third-floor balcony, beaming down at the crowd below as he once more rang the triangle he was holding aloft. His cheeks had a rosy glow that seemed to speak more of a laughing nature than an excess of alcohol, as his eyes were bright but not addled. The woman at his right elbow was more than a head shorter than he and much rounder in the face. She lingered back, the smile on her face a shy one. They exchanged a glance of affectionate warmth, and I was certain she was Ivy's mother.

And the woman to his left must be Ivy herself. Her face was flush with excitement and happiness, and she couldn't stop smiling. She would catch one person's and then another's eye in the crowd and give a little wave and mouth a few words I couldn't decipher, or a wink and a laugh. Her long blonde hair was in an updo, the bangs a perfect arrangement of finger waves, and her ivory dress was nearly as flirty in its flapper style as Sophie's.

There was a young man standing just behind Ivy, looking off to his left towards the upstairs corridor and not down to the crowd below.

It wasn't Edward.

"Squeeze in tight, everyone!" Ivy's father said. He had a booming voice like Santa Claus despite the lack of a single silver hair on his head.

"There you are!" Sophie cried as she and Brianna emerged from the crowd ahead of us as if forced out by all the people surging forward. Brianna pressed up close against my side then moved a bit past me to stand with her back to the wall. She looked a bit pale, and she was hugging herself tightly, hands over her elbows as if worried she might poke them into someone inadvertently. Sophie tripped over someone's foot, although with her usual grace she was already recovering before Otto lunged forward to catch her. "Hello, Otto," she said as he pulled her to her feet and tucked her close beside him.

"Miss Sophie," he said, touching the brim of his hat.

Then someone else emerged from the press of human bodies: Mary. She reached out towards Brianna, who caught her hands and helped her get closer to the wall.

"Amanda, this is Mary Taylor, Charlotte's sister," Brianna said as Mary was thrust against me by the crowd.

"We met," I said. "I guess we're about to discover the big secret."

"Yes," Mary said, bending forward a bit as she fixed a minor disarray of her hair.

Then she looked up towards the top of the stairs, and the expression on her face froze. It was like I could see the blood draining out of it.

"Mary, are you all right?" I asked.

She didn't seem to have even heard me. Brianna was looking at her face as well. It was as if the shock in Mary's face dispelled Brianna's own anxieties, and her body stopped drawing in on itself. She put a hesitant arm on Mary's shoulder.

"Mary?" she asked.

"Oh," Mary said as if coming out of a spell. She looked at Brianna then at me. Her lips parted to speak, but the words died away as Ivy's father's voice once more boomed throughout the hallway.

"We are so pleased to see you all here with us this New Year's Eve!" he said, and Mary gave us a quick apologetic smile that didn't reach her eyes then turned to fix her attention on him. "And not just to help us ring in the new year. No, we also have a special announcement to make!"

"Worst kept secret of the year!" someone in the crowd shouted, and many laughed, including Mr. McTavet himself.

"Yes, indeed!" he said. "Ivy has never been a great keeper of secrets, as many of you are all too well aware!"

Another wave of laughter washed over the hall. But I was distracted. The man behind Ivy had taken half a step towards the corridor and seemed to be trying to communicate something to someone out of sight. Who was this man?

And where was Edward?

I looked over Sophie's head at Otto, putting that question in my eyes. Otto glanced around then gave me a shrug, unconcerned. I gave him a little frown to chastise him. All thoughts of his friend clearly went out of his head the moment Sophie was in view.

"But perhaps this announcement may come as a bit of a surprise for many of you after all," Mr. McTavet said and turned to smile at his daughter. She stepped closer to the balcony, resting her hands on the railing. One hand clutched a little spray of hothouse flowers. The other was sporting a diamond so large we could all see it quite clearly from below.

There was no way Edward would ever have afforded that. Was it a family piece?

"It is with regret that I tell all of the fine young men here, many of whom I've gotten to know quite well over the last few years of visits and earnest conversations about their prospects, that my beautiful Ivy is no longer on the market, as it were."

Ivy flushed a pretty shade of rose. I'm not sure if it's possible to fake a blush, but there was something a touch contrived about her gesture. Not that she was lying, exactly. More like she was playing it up for the crowd.

Mr. McTavet whispered something to Ivy, and she turned to look back at the young man behind her. She waved at him, and he nodded then looked down the corridor again. Who was he talking to? Edward seemed the most logical person, but why was he lingering in the upstairs corridor and not standing at his betrothed's side?

Then the man shook his head, causing his dark brown locks to fall over his forehead. He brushed them back with his fingers then stepped forward to take Ivy's extended hand.

Beside me, Mary made a little choking sound. Brianna and I reached out for her, but she pushed us both away, turning to shove her way back through the crowd in the ballroom doorway. Brianna and I exchanged a glance then Brianna tucked her elbows back in her hands and pushed her way after Mary.

People were already applauding, whistling and hooting, and I had no idea what was going on.

"Who is that man?" I asked Otto. Otto shrugged.

"It is with great pleasure. I announce that my lovely daughter Ivy shall this June become the bride of this very fine young gentleman, Thomas Weingarten!" Mr. McTavet said and started another round of applause.

I looked at Otto again to see if that name meant anything to him. He shrugged again, but concern was starting to edge into his eyes now.

I felt it too. Where was Edward?

"Where's Brianna?" Sophie asked.

"She went to see if Mary was all right," I said.

"What happened to Mary?" she asked.

"I don't know," I said. "I think she knows this Thomas Weingarten.

She was quite upset when she realized he was the betrothed and not Edward."

"Where *is* Edward?" Sophie asked as if none of the rest of us had been thinking it.

"I'm going to look upstairs," I said. "Thomas was talking to someone before he stepped forward. Maybe it was Edward."

"Or Edward skipped the party," Sophie said. "Goodness knows I would."

"Let's look upstairs," Otto said.

"Everyone, move through to the ballroom," Mr. McTavet said in his sonorous voice. "Join us in a dance and a slice of rum cake. And of course, endless glasses of champagne!"

The crowd roared its approval of that plan and stampeded towards the ballroom doors. Otto, Sophie still held tight in his arms, tugged my elbow to pull me out of the rush of bodies, back against the wall. I still got my toes trod on, three times by the heavy flatness of male shoes, but once more painfully from the heel of a woman's shoe that felt far too spiky for 1927.

"If he knew this was happening, wouldn't he have told you?" I asked, my mouth close to Otto's ear to be heard over the boisterousness around us.

"If Coco had known before this very afternoon, it wouldn't still be a secret," Sophie said. "I think this was a last-minute changeup."

It felt that way to me too. But what a horrid idea, to throw someone over for another on the very day you were going to announce your engagement. Maybe not quite as bad as abandoning someone at the altar, although with so many witnesses in attendance, really, not much better.

I had my head down, Otto still inching me and Sophie further away from the door to avoid the unrelenting crowd, but a flutter of motion caught my attention, and I looked up.

Too late to see anything. And if there was a thump, I never heard it.

But then a woman screamed, quickly joined by others, and the crowd started to stampede for real. Otto put his other arm around me and pulled me close, but the press of people trying to get out of the middle of the hall was still crushing. I couldn't breathe. I felt trapped, like there was no air.

I closed my eyes and forced myself to focus on calmness as a concept until my heart stopped pounding so hard and I could draw breath again.

Then I opened my eyes and looked towards the middle of the hall. The parquet floor was a mess of lost top hats and dropped beaded bags, sticky puddles of champagne and a smashed glass or two.

At first, I couldn't make sense of the pool of ivory fabric lumped at the bottom of the stairs. Had a table turned over, the pristine cloth now stained with red wine?

But I hadn't seen a single waiter serving red wine. Only champagne.

Then a sparkle caught my eye. Not broken glass. A diamond. A diamond ring on one finger of an outstretched hand, the hand attached to an arm that was bent at a funny angle.

Then a shriek split the air, a woman's voice screaming Ivy's name in a long, sustained wail that ended in hysterical sobs.

Ivy. I wasn't looking at a broken table crushed by the panicking crowd. I was looking at what remained of Ivy McTavet, lying like a broken and discarded doll across the honey gold wood of the parquet floor.

CHAPTER 6

*M*rs. McTavet's sobs were the only sound echoing through the hallway for what felt like an agonizing eternity. I couldn't take my eyes off that outstretched hand.

It wasn't like she was reaching towards me for help. It was like, even broken and bloody; she wanted me to admire her rock.

Sometimes I hate the thoughts that run through my own head.

Then I heard a stomping noise and looked up to see Mr. McTavet racing down the stairs at what seemed an unwise speed, reeling and stumbling and barely catching himself on the banister.

"John!" he cried. "John, help me!"

I looked around to see who John was. The butler, perhaps? But the butler was leaning against the doorway that led to the foyer, a shaking hand pressed over his eyes, not reacting to Mr. McTavet's cries.

"Let me through," someone said from within the ballroom, and the crowd parted to let one of the tuxedoed men past. He pulled off his top hat and handed it to the younger man following close on his heels before kneeling down beside Ivy's outstretched hand.

"Did she fall?" the man named John asked as Mr. McTavet huffed and puffed down the last flight of stairs.

"I don't know," he said, out of breath. But his voice also had a wavery quality to it, like he'd gladly sink down into hysterical sobs as his wife was still doing up at the top of the stairs.

"You were right beside her," John said.

"Not just then," he said. "I had turned to speak to my wife. Ivy was behind me. I didn't see."

I looked up the stairs. Thomas Weingarten was standing there as if he didn't know what to do or where to go. His face was ashen, and I suspected whatever was going through his head was more primal than actual thoughts.

He was quite close to the balcony railing, though. It was higher than his waist, and Ivy had been quite a bit shorter than he. I doubted very much she could have fallen over that railing by mistake.

The crowd around me had been intense and frightening for the brief time when everyone had been moving at once, but there had only been a few people up on that balcony with her. Her parents, Thomas, and whoever Thomas had been attempting to speak to.

"We should get up there," I said to Otto. Otto nodded, and we tried to slip along the wall, circling around the men standing around Ivy's body, but the third unnamed man noticed us just as we reached the bottom of the stairs and rushed to block our way.

"Stop right there," he said, putting a hand on Otto's chest. Otto narrowed his eyes.

"What's that, Stuart?" John asked, still examining the floor around the body.

"We need to take control of the crime scene, chief," Stuart said, not taking his eyes off the three of us. John, apparently the chief of police, looked up.

"Quite right," he said. He looked towards the ballroom at some of the young men lingering in the doorway. "McConnell, Ricci, get the rest of the boys. We need men on every door. No one comes or goes until we know what happened here."

"It wasn't an accident, sir?" one of the young men asked.

"That's to be determined," the chief said, but his frown said he knew the answer would be no. "McTavet, how many doors are there?"

He had to ask twice before Mr. McTavet heard him. When he

answered his voice sounded odd, like someone speaking while in a hypnotic trance. "Four. Front door, two back doors that open out onto the patio, and the kitchen door."

"Two men on each door, and two more at each end of the upstairs corridor," the chief said to the men in the doorway. "And keep everyone else in the ballroom for now."

"That includes you three," Stuart said to us.

"Our friend is still upstairs," I said, although I didn't know if that was true.

"If that's so, we'll have some questions for your friend," Stuart said. "What's her name?"

"His name is Edward Scott," Otto said.

"Edward?" Mr. McTavet said, as if the name awoke him from his trance. Then his face went through a series of transformations as if a dozen emotions were warring for prominence.

"Is Edward upstairs, Jim?" the chief asked. The blustery command voice he had used on the men in the doorway was now the soft tone of a man speaking to a grieving friend.

"He was," Mr. McTavet said. "Not just now, no. But earlier. Ivy... had to... have words... to explain..." But the words were lost in racking sobs.

"Yes, of course," the chief said. He rested a hand on his friend's shoulder. "Jim, you should see to your wife. She needs you."

"My Ivy," Mr. McTavet sobbed. His hands fluttered around her as if he longed to gather her up in his arms but was also afraid to touch her.

"I'll see to Ivy, Jim," the chief said. He looked around until his eyes found the butler. As if he felt that gaze on him, the butler lowered his hand and pulled himself back into a formal posture. "Tompkins, isn't it? Tompkins, bring Mr. McTavet to the library and get him something to drink. And send someone to see to Mrs. McTavet."

"Of course," Tompkins said. He discreetly wiped at his eyes as he brushed past us to reach Mr. McTavet's side and help him to his feet.

"You three. Where were you when she fell?" the chief asked us.

"Just there, against the wall," Otto said, pointing out the spot.

"Can anyone confirm that?"

"Yes," I said. "We were with Brianna Collins and Mary Taylor."

"Mary," the chief said, the bluster falling out of his voice again as he looked down at Ivy's body. He seemed to be a close friend of her father's. He had probably known her since she was a baby. I couldn't imagine what he was feeling now, still trying to do his job.

But when he looked back to us, his face was all sternly professional once more. "Is someone with Mary now?"

"Brianna," I said. Not that the name would mean anything to the chief. But he nodded.

"It's going to be a while before you can go upstairs or see your friend. For now, I'll ask you to join the others in the ballroom and be as much comfort to Mary as you can."

"Of course," I said. Sophie was also nodding. Otto said nothing at all, although he appeared to be having some sort of staring contest with the policeman named Stuart. Sophie had to drag him away, back to the ballroom.

"I don't like this," Otto said as soon as we were past the young men guarding the door between the ballroom and the hall.

"It's positively horrid," Sophie said.

"I don't mean the murder," Otto said. "I mean what's going to happen next."

"What's going to happen next?" I asked.

"They're going to catch a killer," Otto said. "And if they can't find one, they'll make one."

"Edward?" I said. "But he wasn't even up there."

"You don't really believe the facts are going to matter?" Otto sneered.

"They will if I have anything to say about it," I said.

"*Do* you have anything to say about it?" He was looking at me quite intently, and I knew the question had not been rhetorical.

"We need to find a place to talk," Sophie said. "Just the three of us." Otto was nodding and looking around, but Sophie put a hand on his arm until he looked down at her again. "Not you. The two of us and Brianna."

"Oh. Of course," he said and tapped the side of his nose.

"Can you find her and tell her we're in the parlor?" I asked.

"Will it be quiet there?" Sophie asked.

"If it isn't filled with women overcome with shock or recovering from a light trampling from that crowd," I said. Then more seriously, "It's in the back of the house. If it's occupied, we can find another room there."

"I see red hair," Otto said. "I'll send her after you."

"Thank you, Otto," Sophie said. He nodded then used his dispersal powers to clear a way through the crowd towards the stage for the band at the far end of the room.

Sophie and I slipped out the unguarded doors between the ballroom and the back of the house then down the semi-dark corridor to the parlor. I was surprised to find it empty, but then the people standing in the ballroom were largely in such a deep state of shock and numbness they looked like they'd only move about if led by others.

"I'm here," Brianna said as she came in the door, also looking around to be sure we were alone. "Are we leaving?"

"We can't," I said.

"We can evade a police guard, surely," Sophie said. Brianna lifted her eyebrows at that comment.

"We have to stay," I said. "If Otto is right and they try to pin this on Edward, we're going to have to intervene. Or, I guess, I will."

"We," Sophie said, crossing her arms. "Whatever we decide, we do together."

"It wasn't an accident, then? Brianna asked. "I didn't see exactly what happened."

"I didn't either," I said. We both looked at Sophie, who shook her head.

"But even if it was murder, surely that's a matter for the police," Brianna said. "Isn't it?"

"I would tend to agree with that assessment," Sophie said, looking to me.

"I would too," I said, although it almost hurt getting the words out.

"As corrupt as Otto says they are, surely that's just in matters dealing with prohibition and the gangs and that. The murder of the daughter of a prominent family is surely another thing altogether."

"So what are we doing?" Brianna asked.

"We're being sure," I said, "that magic wasn't involved."

"Each in our own way?" Sophie asked. "Like before?"

"Yes, but I guess we can't really all go to separate rooms this time," I said.

"I can tune you out," Sophie said, then turned to move one of the little tea tables out of the way so she could have enough room to dance.

"I'll be over here," Brianna said, moving towards a little nook lined with bookcases. They didn't really look like Brianna's sort of books, but I guessed she was just drawn to the smell of ink and paper and binding glue.

I dropped to the floor with my back against the wall, the skirts of my sapphire gown ballooning around me then slowly sinking to the floor. I closed my eyes and switched my awareness to the other place, to the world of threads.

I had never done this with so many minds in such close proximity to mine. I had spread my awareness over city blocks before, but that had been a different experience. This was more concentrated. I could feel everyone's shock and grief, a wave of emotion that nearly staggered me. I was only vaguely aware of my physical form, but I could feel the tickle of tears running down my cheeks.

Then I left my body behind entirely, moving past the knots of souls in the ballroom to the hall itself. I could see the dying light from the threads that made Ivy. Her story was coming to an end, although it was continuing on a bit past her last breath. She was connected to everything around her. To her father at the back of the house. To her mother in a room at the front of the house on the second floor. To Thomas still standing at the top of the staircase as if he had become petrified.

To Edward, alone in a tiny room at the end of the third-floor corridor. I passed my mind over the threads that formed Edward, feeling his confusion and fear and sadness and anger.

I wished there was a way to make him feel me, to know that I was there, to lend him some measure of comfort.

But if there were, it was a magic I didn't yet know.

I went back to my body and opened my eyes. Brianna and Sophie were both sitting on the floor in front of me, waiting.

"Nothing," I said.

"Nothing," Sophie said.

"No, nothing at all," Brianna said. "Not Evanora, not any sort of enchanted object or remnant of a spell. Not even some rogue energy flowing out from one of us."

"You checked for that?" I asked. "I didn't even know that was a thing."

"It's rare, but definitely a thing," she said. "But it didn't happen here. Despite our presence, and the fact that at least one witch is in this time period looking to make trouble, whatever happened to Ivy was, if not an accident, still a perfectly natural event."

"So we stay out of it," Sophie said, looking at me. Not a question.

"We stay out of it," I said.

But to myself, I added, "for now."

CHAPTER 7

*W*hen we rejoined the others in the ballroom, I was surprised to find that the band, just like the one on board the *Titanic*, played on. Not rollicking dance numbers, but something soft and melancholy yet not quite funereal. They seemed to be playing more for themselves than for the others gathered in the room, but that only made it that much more moving to me.

"Where did you leave Mary?" I asked, rising up on tiptoe to try to see over the crowd. Impossible with all of the top hats.

"Leave her?" Brianna asked.

"Weren't you with her when Otto found you?" I asked.

"No," she said. I turned to look at her, as did Sophie. Brianna flinched back from that much direct gaze, immediately looking down at the toes of her shoes. "I followed her out of the hall. She ran across the ballroom, and I ran after, but I lost her in those back halls."

"They aren't all that confusing," Sophie said.

"She was probably going to the parlor," I said.

"No," Brianna said. "That was the one room with open doors, so I found it right away, but she wasn't there."

"So where did she go?" Sophie asked.

"Where is she now?" I asked. We all looked around. With her brown hair and sedate dress, she wouldn't exactly jump out of the background. But even a careful search didn't turn her up.

I did see Otto speaking to a balding man in a tuxedo that had probably fit him better a few years before. Otto saw me looking his way and gave me a little nod but kept his attention on what the man was saying to him.

"Mary was upset about the announcement," I said. "And she knows this house well. She and Ivy have been friends forever. There must be all sorts of places a girl can hide to have a cry and no one can find her."

"If she hid before Ivy fell..." Sophie began but didn't finish her thought.

"Surely she heard the commotion," Brianna said.

"We really should find her," I said.

"There must be back stairs like we have at the charm school," Brianna said. "Servant stairs even."

"Let's just try the main stair first," Sophie said, adjusting her skirt and then her hair. Not that either needed any attention.

"The police chief did seem to have a soft spot for Mary," I said. "And he did ask us specifically to see to her."

Brianna nodded her agreement with the plan, and the three of us slipped through the clustered groups of shocked partygoers to the double doors that still stood open out onto the hall. Two police officers were standing, one on either side of the door. The younger of the two with thick blond hair that had resisted his efforts at combing it back was unfamiliar to me, but the slightly older one with red hair just beginning to recede from the sides of his forehead was either McConnell or Ricci.

I opened my mouth to speak, but Sophie brushed past me, putting a hand on the red-headed officer's arm. Just a few fingertips barely brushing his sleeve, but she had his attention at once.

"Officer McConnell?" she asked.

"Yes?" he said.

"We can't find Mary in the ballroom or the parlor. We think she's still upstairs. Alone. Distraught. Can you just let us up the stairs to look for her?" Sophie asked.

"We'll walk around the sides of the room," I said. I wasn't sure what the protocol was for crime scenes in 1927 except for certainly far less stringent than 2018.

McConnell gave us a studious frown as he mulled it over. The other officer was watching him closely to see what he decided.

"Where exactly are you going to look for her?" he asked.

"Ivy's bedroom," I said. As if we even knew where that was.

"We're terribly worried that she doesn't even know what happened to Ivy," Sophie said. "No one has seen her since before the fall."

"Truly?" McConnell asked us. We all nodded gravely.

He was just stepping aside to let us out of the ballroom when a door across the hall slammed, and the staccato beat of boot heels echoed through the space. McConnell quickly thrust his arm out to stop Sophie from brushing past him before looking over his shoulder at the approaching officer. It was Stuart.

"What's going on here?" He asked as he stopped in front of McConnell.

"They need to go upstairs to find Mary Taylor. She's not on the first floor," McConnell said.

"No need," Stuart said. "She's in the library." He gave Sophie an appraising look. Then his gaze skipped quickly over Brianna to linger on me. "Didn't you say she was with you?"

"No," I said. "We haven't been able to find her."

"Yes, you did," he said, thrusting his hands in his pockets and rocking back on his heels. "When the chief asked you where you were when Ivy fell, you said you were against that wall with Mary Taylor."

"I was," I said. "Mary *was* there with me, but she left just before Ivy fell."

"Huh," Stuart said, still rocking back and forth on his feet. I didn't like the triumphant look in his eye, like he'd caught me in a lie. "So now it's Mary you're looking for upstairs. Just a few minutes ago you desperately needed to get upstairs to find your friend Edward Scott. Maybe you should just tell me what it is you really need to get upstairs for."

"If we're your best suspects, your investigation really is in trouble," Sophie said. Stuart gave her a dark look that edged a little too close to a "why is this one talking to me" look for my taste. I felt my hands curling into fists.

But apparently I was doing more than that, things I wasn't aware of until Brianna seized my arm and gave it a fierce squeeze. I unfisted my hands, but it was also like some wind that had been blowing through my hair and billowing out the skirt of my gown died down at the same moment.

What had I been doing?

Brianna's green eyes were wide with alarm. I patted her hand still on my arm, the only way I could promise her to be more careful.

"Can we please just see to Mary?" I asked.

"No need," Stuart said. His voice sort of underlined those words, and I remembered he had said the same thing to McConnell just a moment before. "She's in the library."

"Where's the library?" Brianna asked breathlessly. She really couldn't help herself.

"Off limits," Stuart said firmly. "You should rejoin the others in the ballroom for now. Get some food. The kitchen is going to be bringing out coffee in a moment to sober you all up."

I scoffed. Minutes before he had been a partygoer himself, and I would bet he had drunk his fair share of the champagne.

Stuart glared at me for a moment before speaking again. "Just wait with the others. Witnesses will be called to give their statements in the library as the chief and the detectives require them. And I'm just sure your three names will come up."

"When they're done with Mary?" I prompted.

"She'll be sent out to join the others," Stuart said. "No one is going to be wandering this house until we get to the bottom of this."

"And Edward?" I asked.

"Is in custody," Stuart said firmly. "He's been questioned and will likely be questioned again. But he won't be joining the party."

"He's your chief suspect then?" Sophie asked, and didn't flinch when he pinned that dark gaze back on her.

"One of two," Stuart said.

"Thomas?" I guessed.

Now he was back to glaring at me. "The details of the investigation are not for public dissemination."

I opened my mouth to say something sarcastic about all of the details he had just disseminated to us when Brianna squeezed my arm again and I let it go.

Sophie gave him one last long look before turning on her heel, tossing her beaded bag over one shoulder, and strolling off toward the buffet table.

Brianna and I followed her, less impressively.

But when we caught up with her at the table, she was just standing over the display of food, hands making and releasing fists over and over again, her breath coming in angry jags.

"He was unspeakably rude to you," Brianna said.

"Nothing I haven't dealt with before," Sophie said through gritted teeth. She took a deep cleansing breath and untensed her whole body, then picked up a plate and started piling it with food as if this were the most relaxing party in the world.

"You're still hungry?" I asked.

Sophie shrugged. "We can all pick at it," she said, then thrust a shrimp cocktail into my hands.

"Should we go back to the parlor where we can talk freely?" Brianna asked.

"No, I want to look at people," Sophie said. "Besides, if we're not here when they call our names, they'll count that as a mark against us."

"We really shouldn't let them question us," I said. "Events of the party, fine. But if they start asking more questions about who we are and why we're here-"

"We lie," Sophie said with a shrug. Plate full, she looked around and found a little standing table no one was using. It was close to the band who were still softly playing a song that made me think of autumn leaves and long, cold nights. Sophie set her plate down, gave the band a little wave that they returned with nods, and then turned to wave Brianna and me closer.

"If we're letting the police solve this, which we should absolutely do, why are we staying?" Brianna asked.

"Especially if they're planning on questioning us, she might have a point," Sophie said, dipping a shrimp in the cocktail sauce.

"I'm not leaving until I know they aren't pinning this on Edward," I said.

"Maybe he is involved, though," Sophie said. She held up a hand at my furious glare. "I'm not saying he's a murderer. Clearly, we know he's not. Not coldblooded, anyway. But what if there was a scuffle? Two men grappling with each other could knock a woman of Ivy's size over the railing. Especially if she tried to intervene."

"I didn't hear a scuffle," I said.

"But it was loud at that moment," Sophie said. "Everyone was moving towards the ballroom, nearly trampling us as they went by. Talking, laughing, breaking glasses, apparently. Would we have heard it even if it had happened?"

"All right, say they did grapple with each other. Wouldn't we then have seen Edward at the top of the stairs and not just Thomas?" I asked.

"If that's what happened, it would be as much Thomas' fault as Edward's," Brianna said.

"I don't believe for a minute that's what happened," I said firmly. "Edward isn't a murderer. He also isn't a... scuffler. I don't see him doing it. I'm sure he had a lot of feelings about being thrown over for this other man, but I just don't see him acting on it in that way."

"You never really know what a person will do in extreme circumstances until you test them," Sophie said.

"And then it's too late," Brianna said.

I stepped away from the table. Not far, just a few steps, but I needed a moment to process.

Did they really not see Edward in the same eyes I did? Despite his upbringing, there wasn't a bit of roughness to his character. He wasn't a bit like... Otto, I guess.

When my brain is busy, my feet like to pace, and I started walking around the perimeter of the room, twisting my beaded bag between my hands. I caught snatches of conversation around me, but I was tuning the voices out until I started hearing Edward's name.

I slowed my steps, listening but keeping my head down, looking at the bag in my hands. I didn't want to attach faces to those voices. Not now, when I was this angry.

And it almost didn't matter who was speaking since they were all saying the same things. Came from a bad family. Came from no family. Pretended to be "one of us" but clearly never was. Rough manners. Rougher friends.

No one mentioned Thomas' name except in the sense that he was also a victim, having lost his betrothed.

No one had any real evidence, and yet every one of them had come to the same conclusion. Edward was guilty.

My route around the room brought me back to the table were Brianna and Sophie were still talking together in whispers. I came back to the table and slammed my bag down on the table.

"Everyone agrees with you, apparently," I said, crossing my arms. "Edward is guilty, and that is that."

"We didn't say that," Brianna said. "In an investigation, it's important to examine all the angles, even the painful ones."

"But we're not the ones investigating, are we?" I asked. "No, we agreed to let the police take this one. And here we are, standing on the sidelines while they botch it."

"Amanda," Sophie said, putting a hand on mine and giving it a squeeze. "These fine people waiting in this room with us are not the police. The police are in the library, questioning everyone and gathering the stories to compare. They're all over the rest of the house, gathering what clues they can. We have to let them do it."

"For now?" I asked.

Sophie gave me a grave nod. "For now. If they really do botch it..."

She ended in a noncommittal shrug and popped another square of cheese in her mouth.

But with her other hand, she was tapping her beaded bag, on the table next to mine. Her bag, like mine and like Brianna's, was long and narrow to accommodate the one item we all three carried that the rest of the women in attendance didn't have.

Our wands.

CHAPTER 8

I love coffee. In particular, I love the smell of coffee. Even after years of working in a diner that was thick with the aroma of brewing coffee and fried food, I never tired of it.

It wasn't even just from working there. I had grown up in that diner, sitting in the kitchen watching my mother as she washed dishes and unpacked boxes from the supplier and made pot after pot of coffee. It wouldn't be an exaggeration to say that smell permeated my entire childhood. I'm sure even when I was home I could still smell it on my clothes and my mother's.

Now that I lived at the charm school, the smell of that coffee had changed. Mr. Trevor favored a dark roast, with its richer aroma. But he only made a pot in the morning, and when that was gone, we all drank tea.

I hadn't realized how much my brain had adjusted to the smell of coffee meaning my meditation practice was done, but I hadn't yet started the real challenge of my work in the library.

In short, coffee meant mornings to me now. And I hadn't even noticed that shift until I stood looking down at the half-drunk cup sitting on the table in front of me as the clock inched closer to midnight. Coffee at night hadn't been odd before. It was definitely unsettling now.

Brianna touched my hand, and I looked up to see McConnell waving to catch our attention. A woman was standing next to him with her head down, her brown hair hanging loose and covering her face. I recognized the dress. It was Mary Taylor.

I rushed over to put an arm around her, and McConnell gave me a look of deep gratitude. Clearly, he had no clue what to do to calm a distraught young woman and was happy to hand her over to me.

"Do you want to go to the parlor where it's quiet?" I asked Mary. She wasn't crying at the moment, but her red-rimmed eyes said she had been doing plenty of it in the recent past.

"No," she said. "I just need to sit."

"Of course," I said. I guided her across the room to where Sophie had found a chair and Brianna had produced a cup of tea out of seemingly nowhere. Mary sat primly in the chair and took the tea from Brianna with a murmur of thanks.

"We lost track of you in all of the commotion," I said.

"Sorry. I just needed a moment to myself," Mary said. Then looked up at us, eyes widening. "Oh dear. I hope I didn't worry you all? That wasn't my intention."

"We just wanted to be sure you were all right," I said. "You seemed very upset when you left the hall."

"Did the police tell you about Ivy?" Sophie asked. "I hope they did it gently."

"They did, but I already knew," Mary said, looking down at the tea in her hands. "After I left the hall I went upstairs. I wanted to talk to... it doesn't matter. But I was there, coming down the corridor, when... it happened."

We three exchanged excited glances. This was news. "What did you see?" I asked.

"Nothing helpful," Mary said, pressing a trembling hand to her forehead. "I saw people on the balcony, but the light from the hall was too bright. The chandelier is level with the third floor. You can't really tell if you look up from below, but when you're up there, it's a bit blinding."

"Do you know who was there?" I asked.

"Ivy," Mary said. Her voice threatened to catch, and she paused for a moment until she had her emotions back under control. "Her parents. Thomas. Edward." I flinched. "And Coco and Charlotte."

"Coco and Charlotte?" I asked. It wasn't until she said their names that I realized I hadn't once thought of either of them since before the big announcement. I hadn't seen them with the other guests during the announcement or after.

"They weren't on the balcony," Sophie said.

"No," Mary said. She looked up at me. "At the end of the upstairs hall is a playroom. Just a tiny space too small for an adult to stand up in. You get in through a little door even a child has to crawl through. Sort of a hidden panel in the woodwork of the wall at the top of the steps. When I got far enough down the hall to see people as more than silhouettes against the light, Coco and Charlotte were there, by that door. I guess they had been hiding in the playroom and were drawn out by the noise."

"But where are they now?" I asked. I looked around the ballroom even though I was quite certain they were not there.

"I'm not sure," Mary said. "I haven't seen them since."

"What happened right after?" I asked. Brianna gave me a nudge, and I realized that my tone was probably pretty grilling, and Mary had just been grilled by actual police for the better part of an hour. "I'm sorry. It's just, no one will let us see Edward. You said he was there?"

"He was," Mary said. "I was walking down the hall towards the balcony when I heard Ivy cry out. But I couldn't see anything. Then everyone below was shouting, and I started to run. When I got to the balcony, Mrs. McTavet was collapsed on the floor. Thomas was standing there like he'd been turned to stone. He didn't even look at me when I called his name." She looked down at her tea again. A single tear splashed down into its milky depths.

"And Edward?" Sophie asked softly.

"Edward was actually coming towards me," Mary said. "I stopped short of the balcony, still in the corridor but close enough to see clearly. Edward was backing away, sort of reeling. He didn't turn until he collided with me. Then he sort of stumbled drunkenly down the corridor behind me. I don't know where he was going."

"He was drunk?" I asked, surprised.

"No, no," Mary said. "I just meant, he didn't seem to be all there. Shock, I imagine. Shock," she repeated, and her eyes were back on her tea. "He really did love Ivy very, very much. I can't imagine the shock he must be feeling. Twice in a day." The tea on her lap began to tremble, and Brianna hastened to remove it before Mary collapsed into tears. Sophie put an arm around her, turning her own body to block the view of anyone else in the room who might be inclined to gawk.

I caught Brianna's eye and tipped my head towards a corner of the room. She nodded, setting the cup on one of the tables, then joined me.

"We should find Coco and Charlotte," I said. "If they were there the entire time, they might have seen what happened."

"Maybe the police are questioning them right now," Brianna said. She didn't say the words, but by her tone, I knew she was reminding me that we had agreed to let the police solve this crime.

"We're Coco's guests," I said. "We should be sure she's all right."

"So you want to go back to the police guarding the door and tell them you have to get upstairs, this time to see yet a third person?" Brianna asked.

"What, you don't think they'd be up for that?" I asked sarcastically then sighed. "You're right. They'll only be more suspicious of us if I ask."

"And we're trying to avoid attention," she reminded me.

"So we don't ask the same police officers," I said. "There's a pair guarding the back stairs that don't even know who we are."

"Unless they've been warned we might try to get upstairs again," Brianna said.

"Can't they at least look for the girls themselves and send them down to us?" I asked. "Charlotte should be with her sister just now."

"Agreed," Brianna said, looking past me to where Mary was once more drying her eyes and nodding at whatever words Sophie was whispering to her. "But perhaps Coco isn't here because she's with her mother?"

"I hadn't thought of that," I admitted. "But I do really wish she were here. She's probably the only one besides the three of us who has any feeling for Edward. And maybe she saw enough to prove his innocence."

"She *is* fond of Edward," Brianna said. "If Mary told the police what she just told us, they're going to be talking to Coco at some point. And Coco won't let them say a bad thing about Edward; you know she won't."

"She *is* loyal," I said.

"And precocious," Brianna said. "She's not going to be talked out of what she believes, not even by a room full of grownups who are also police."

"I agree," I said, then took a breath. "Thanks, I feel better now. Hope is nice. Do you imagine she'll come in here when the police are done talking to her?"

"Or maybe sooner," Brianna said and nodded her head towards the back door to the ballroom, the one that led towards the parlor.

Coco was standing in the doorway looking around the room. When her sweeping gaze finally reached us, she rose up on tiptoe and waved. Then she turned back towards the darkened hall behind her, catching someone by the arm to drag them after her across the ballroom.

It was Charlotte, of course. Looking as surly as ever. But then she saw her older sister talking with Sophie, twisting a well-used handkerchief in her hands, and that surly look melted into one of genuine concern.

Coco made a beeline towards Brianna and me, but Charlotte went straight to her sister, who burst into fresh tears as she got up from the chair to gather her little sister into a tight embrace.

"How are you doing?" I asked as Coco stopped in front of Brianna and me.

"Oh," Coco said, blinking repeatedly and staring up into the light rather than looking at either of us. "Oh. Not good."

"And your mother?" Brianna asked.

"Really not good," Coco said, blinking more fiercely than ever.

"Why don't we get out of this room to somewhere more private," I said.

"I'm all right," Coco said. A bubble in her throat was making her voice sound unusually deep.

"You don't have to be," I said. "You've had a terrible shock. It's perfectly normal for you to be not all right."

Coco nodded but was still blinking back tears.

"Do you need anything?" Brianna asked. "Tea or something to eat? Maybe a chair?"

"Just one thing," Coco said. A fierceness was in her voice now, and the blinking had stopped. She gave us each a hard look, first Brianna and then me.

"What is it?" Brianna asked. She was half-opening her bag, as if she were about to pull out her wand and magic up whatever Coco asked for, there in front of the band and everyone.

Coco leaned forward, and it was like someone had just poured gasoline on the fire in her eyes, flaring it up to vicious life.

"Justice," she said.

CHAPTER 9

*B*rianna and I didn't know what to say to that. Of course, she would want justice for her sister, that wasn't odd. But the way she was looking at the two of us, it was as if she expected us to deliver it for her.

But she didn't know that we were witches. So what exactly was she asking us to do?

"The police are being very thorough," Brianna said, and I could tell by the unusually slow pace of her words that she was choosing them carefully.

"No, they aren't," Coco said. "They've already decided it was Edward, and they aren't asking the right questions to find out who really did it. They're just convincing everyone who isn't sure what they saw exactly that they saw Edward."

"I'm sure that's not true," Brianna said, then fell back half a step when Coco glared up at her with that fire back in her eyes.

"It's absolutely true," Coco said.

"Did they question you and Charlotte?" I asked.

The question seemed to calm her mind, and some of the anger left her as she shook her head. "No. They haven't even found us. They probably will now that we've come out. Charlotte wanted to see her sister."

"Mary needed her," I said, looking past Coco to where the two sisters were still hugging and rocking each other.

"You were deliberately hiding?" Brianna asked. Coco nodded. "Where? In the playroom upstairs?"

"No," Coco said, not surprised that we knew of its existence. "There's another one downstairs."

"Really?" I said. "Why so many hidden places?"

Coco looked for a moment like she didn't want to tell us, and I wasn't going to press, but then she changed her mind. "My mother is actually my father's second wife. He built this house for his first family. He had two sons then. He built the tunnels through the walls and the hidden playrooms and the treehouse in the backyard all for them."

"You have two older brothers? I had no idea," Brianna said.

"Had," Coco said, and her voice went flat.

"I'm so sorry," I said. "You've lost all of your siblings?"

Coco shrugged, but she was blinking again. "My brothers died in the war. I barely remember them. Ivy did, a little, but she didn't really like talking about them."

My heart broke a little for poor Mr. McTavet. Now he'd buried a first wife and three of his children. Maybe that wasn't as unusual in 1927 as it was in modern times, but it was still a tragedy.

"Anyway," Coco said, her emotions back under firm control. "Charlotte and I were in the cubby behind the library fireplace. We were listening to the police officers talking. But after they finished questioning Mary, Charlotte wanted to go see her. I still wanted to listen, but she can be mean if you don't let her have her way." She cast an annoyed glance over her shoulder at her sometime companion. "If you don't believe me about how they're handling this, we can go in there and listen."

"I believe you," I said. "Who are they questioning now?"

"At the moment they're just talking to each other. They've sent people out to find Otto, but apparently, he's not findable."

I looked around the room and realized that indeed Otto was nowhere to be seen.

"Otto was downstairs with us at the time," I said.

"Like it matters," Coco scoffed. "They aren't asking about the fall. They're digging into Edward's past. I told you, they aren't after justice. They just need someone to take the blame. But I want actual justice."

"So do we," I said.

"Then you need to start looking for clues, right?" Coco said, looking imploringly at us both. "I know you solve murders. You did before with Cynthia Thomas. You figured out it was her sister, and you brought her to justice."

"That was different," Brianna said.

"How?" Coco demanded.

Brianna opened and closed her mouth a few times before summoning up the words, "she worked at the school. So. We had to."

"My sister lived next door to your school," Coco said.

"That's different," Brianna said.

"I'm asking you to," Coco said. "As a friend. Please. I know you can help me. I know you're not like other people even though you pretend you are. I know you can do this if you want to. Why don't you want to?"

"We do want to," I said, ignoring Brianna's warning look. "There are rules we have to follow. We can't break them."

"I break rules all the time," Coco said. "I follow the important ones, but most rules are just stupid. Why would you follow stupid rules?"

"These are important ones," I said. "Coco, I promise, we're going to do all we can to make sure the police don't hurt anyone here. Not Edward or you or anyone. But we can't act unless it's clear that's what's about to happen."

"The chief seems like he's a close friend of your father's," Brianna said.

Coco nodded. "They went to school together."

"Don't you think he wants justice too?" Brianna asked.

Coco mulled it over. "Maybe he would in a normal situation, but this isn't normal." She took a deep breath and glanced around to be sure no one was close enough to overhear, then took a step closer before whispering to us. "I was in that library cubby a week ago when he came to see my father. Ivy was still planning to get engaged to Edward then. But the chief had been digging into Edward's past. I guess he thought he was being a good friend. He told my father all about Edward growing up in an orphanage and how he was still close friends with some young gangster who's been... How did he say it? Gaining notoriety?"

"Otto," I guessed.

"Otto Mayer," Coco said. "Apparently he's done all sorts of illegal things. The chief kept going on and on about it. Then I remembered that one time when I ran into Edward on the corner by the shop, he was with a friend he said was named Otto, so I guess it was the same guy. He didn't look like a gangster. Is he even at the party?"

"Yes," I said. "You'd know him now if you saw him. He's not wearing a black tux."

"The guy in the green suit with the purple vest?" Coco said, and something like a grin touched her lips. "He looked interesting. I didn't recognize him from before. Wow."

"They can't pin this on Otto," I said. "He doesn't have motive, and he was standing next to me the entire time."

"They aren't trying to," Coco said, getting impatient. "They are going to ask him all sorts of questions about Edward's childhood so they can make it seem like he's a thug who tried to marry above his station and turned violent when he failed."

"What did your father say that day when the chief told him about Edward and Otto?" Brianna asked.

"He got mad," Coco said. "My father really liked Edward."

"So what happened?" I asked. "Why did Ivy get engaged to Thomas instead?"

Coco shrugged. "They've known each other forever."

"But when did she change her mind?" I asked.

"Just today," Coco said. "They were setting up for the party, and we were all getting dressed when Thomas came to see her. They went into the parlor for a really long time, and when they came out, the whole plan changed. I don't know what he said to change her mind."

"Surely Edward knew before that announcement?" I asked.

Coco shrugged again. "He came early, but I don't know. I was already on hostess duty with Charlotte Taylor."

"Charlotte came over with Mary?" I asked, and Coco nodded. "Did Mary know then?"

Coco bit at her lip. "I don't know."

"She didn't seem to," I said. "When she saw Thomas up on the balcony with Ivy, it seemed to come to her as a complete surprise."

Coco sunk her teeth deeper into her lip. "Ivy talked to Thomas and mother, mother told me about the change but said it was a secret I wasn't to tell anyone."

"Was your mother happy about the change?"

"Yes, definitely," Coco said. "She always liked Thomas better. But father was cross."

"Because he liked Edward?" I guessed.

Coco flinched when she bit her lip this time. Clearly, she was giving it too much of a workout. "I think he liked them both the same," she decided. "But he didn't like how Ivy was handling things."

"Okay, let's go over it again," I said. "Ivy and Thomas in the parlor with your mother. They come out and announce the change in plans. Then who goes where?"

"My father dragged Thomas into his study and Ivy went upstairs with my mother to finish getting ready," Coco said. "But Mary and Charlotte showed up before we were even up the stairs. Mary went with Ivy and my mother to Ivy's room, and I was stuck with surly Charlotte."

"And Edward?" I asked.

"He came later," Coco said. "And Tompkins took him right into the study where my father and Thomas were. I wanted to listen in, but Charlotte didn't want to."

"So you don't know when Mary knew about the change in betrothals," I said, and Coco nodded. "When did Charlotte know? Did you tell her?"

"I mean," Coco said, her cheeks coloring. "I told her the same thing I told you. That there was a big secret, but I couldn't tell her."

"So she heard it the same time we did when your father announced it?" I asked.

"Yes, but why does that matter?" Coco asked. "What does Charlotte care?"

"Her sister," I said, and Coco looked back over her shoulder to where Mary and Charlotte were sitting in chairs now but still holding hands. "Mary was clearly attached to Thomas. And Charlotte knew she was."

"Yes, but, Charlotte didn't even like Thomas," Coco said. "Not that she really likes anyone besides Mary, but in particular she didn't like Thomas."

"Why?" I asked.

"I don't know," Coco said, throwing up her hands. "You should probably just ask her."

"Maybe not now," I said. Mary looked in better spirits now that her sister was with her. "Did you see what happened up on the balcony?"

"No," she said and started blinking again. "The light up there is so bright. We don't usually have that chandelier all lit up like that. Just for parties."

"Mary told us that Edward was in the corridor," I said.

"He was," Coco said. "The whole time, actually. Thomas wanted him to come out and show there were no hard feelings, but Edward wouldn't go. Then we were all supposed to go downstairs to join the party, but it got confusing. Everyone seemed to be moving at once, and then someone knocked me back into the wall, and I nearly fell down. Then I heard my mother screaming."

"You didn't see Ivy fall?" I asked.

"No. It was too bright," Coco said.

"So the only people on the balcony were you and Charlotte, your parents, Thomas and Ivy?" I asked. "With Mary and Edward in the corridor? No servants or anyone else?"

"No," Coco said, but slowly.

"What is it?" I asked.

"I don't know. I couldn't see well, and then I got knocked down," she said.

"By who?" I asked.

"That's just it. I don't know," she said. "When I got back up, everyone else was right where they had been. Except for Ivy."

"So you don't know who bumped into you?"

"More like shoved me down," Coco said. "But no, I don't know who it was. They were strong."

"So maybe not Charlotte or Mary then?" I asked.

Coco shrugged. "Edward and Thomas were too far away. I think maybe someone else ran up the stairs or something. I definitely wouldn't have been able to see anyone rushing up the stairs with the chandelier all lit up."

I exchanged a glance with Brianna. She hadn't been there at that moment, but I was certain if anyone had been running up the stairs just then, someone would have seen it from below.

"It seems like the only way to clear this up is to talk to Edward and Thomas," Brianna said.

"Have they been taken to the library yet?" I asked.

"No. The chief said they'd question them last," Coco said. "He wanted all of the other stories first so he could catch them if they tried to lie."

"They," I said.

"Yes, he said they, but everyone there knew he meant Edward," Coco said darkly.

"Do you know where they are now?" I asked.

Coco shrugged. "Not here or in the library."

"We should search the house," I said. "They must both be upstairs somewhere."

"They'll just stop us again if we try to go upstairs," Brianna said.

"I can go," Coco said. "I'll look around and figure out where they are and then come get you."

"Perfect," I said. Coco turned to head back out the doors she had come in from when to her surprise as much as mine Charlotte bolted up out of her chair to run after her.

"I'm not sure they're on the same page in terms of their friendship," I said as Coco reluctantly let Charlotte tag along on her mission.

Then Sophie left Mary's side to come over to us. "What's going on?" she asked. "What was Coco telling you?"

"Nothing really concrete," I said. "But they're definitely trying to pin this on Edward."

"So what's the plan?" Sophie asked.

She sounded ready to argue if I wanted to do anything drastic. Which part of me really wanted to. But she and Brianna were right. We needed to keep a low profile.

"We should find Otto," I said. "Before the police do."

CHAPTER 10

$\mathcal{W}$e went through the ballroom, the parlor, the powder room, and up and down all of the corridors in the back of the house, but there was no sign of Otto.

"Did he sneak upstairs?" Brianna asked, looking down the corridor to the pair of officers standing guard there.

"Hold on," I said, sitting down on a chair that was against the wall in the corridor, opposite a set of double doors I was sure went to Mr. McTavet's study. I could hear the murmur of male voices inside. The chair had a stale cigar smell to it and wasn't particularly comfortable, but I only needed a moment.

I closed my eyes and pushed my awareness out of my body. It wasn't hard to find Otto this way. I knew his pattern of threads well after our last adventure together.

I opened my eyes. "He's in the kitchen," I said.

Sophie nodded and looked around, but there was no sign of a kitchen door in our corridor.

"This way," I said, getting up from the chair and leading the way back to the ballroom.

The food on the buffet table was starting to look a little sad, and I was certain anyone who tried to eat one of the shrimp cocktails now was going to have regrets.

Then a waiter went by holding a tray of empty coffee cups. We three watched as he crossed the room, then pushed against what looked like any other panel in the wood-covered walls. It pivoted on unseen hinges, and he disappeared.

"Mr. McTavet certainly likes a bit of mystery," I said. We crept closer to the door and waited to see if anyone was going to come back out of it, but there was no way to tell. Then another waiter came towards us, this one carrying a bin filled with dirty plates. He gave us a little nod as we stepped aside to let him pass.

We waited a beat then Sophie pushed through the door after him. Brianna and I followed.

Now we were standing in a dark room filled with shelves, a bit large for a butler's pantry but clearly the McTavets liked to throw lavish parties. From the other end of the room, we could hear the clatter of dishes and the splashing of wash water as well as many voices conversing in low tones. The pallor over the party extended to the staff as well. Not surprising. Ivy had seemed well liked by everyone.

We crept closer to the light. Sophie peeked into the kitchen then quickly slipped across the open space in front of the door to the butler's pantry, disappearing behind a wall of empty crates that had once held bottles of champagne. Brianna watched for a moment then followed. Then it was my turn to watch the servants gathered at the far end of the room, washing dishes and filling pots with coffee and stacking trays high with clean cups. They were talking together, but discreetly, in low voices with their heads bent together. No one was looking my way.

I followed the others.

The space between the back wall and the champagne crates was darkened like the butler's pantry and narrow. I could see Sophie and Brianna at the far end looking down at something, and when I got closer, I realized they were both standing over Otto, who had made himself a seat out of an overturned crate and was drinking the contents of one of the bottles. Several empties were rolling on the ground at his feet.

"Is this helpful?" I asked him in a furious whisper that was still loud enough to make both Brianna and Sophie gesture with their hands for me to quiet down.

"It wasn't a hit," Otto said, over-enunciating each word.

"Well, who thought it was?" I asked, still a shade too loudly.

"Me," Otto said. "But it isn't. So."

"You thought one of your buddies sent someone up there to push Ivy over the side?" I asked. "Why? The only person here who ever expressed any animosity towards her was you, frankly."

"All I ever said was that she wasn't right for Edward," Otto said, pausing to take yet another gulp of champagne. "And I stand by that assessment."

"When was this?" Sophie asked, but I waved the question aside.

"Otto-" I began, but he made a frustrated sound and kept making it until I stopped trying to speak.

"Your argument makes no sense," he said. "Why would I want her dead the very minute it's revealed that she wasn't even going to marry Edward?"

"Because you didn't know until that minute either?" I said. "It doesn't matter. I wasn't actually accusing you."

"No, I suppose you could just look into my eyes and see my heart," he said, still angry.

"Not exactly," I said.

"Coco thinks there might have been someone else up on the balcony beside the family," Brianna said. "Is that true? Is that why you thought there might be a hitman?"

"I did not know that," Otto said and lurched to one side as he attempted to turn his head to look at her.

"Why would a hitman be after Ivy? You didn't explain that," Sophie said. He lurched again as he turned his attention to her. She bent down and gently took the mostly empty bottle from his hands, setting it on the floor with the others. "Otto, is anyone else in danger?"

"No," he said. "Everyone I spoke to swore they weren't here for business, and I believe them."

"But Ivy-" I began.

"I didn't think she was the target," Otto burst out, prompting Brianna and Sophie to flutter their hands again.

"Someone else then? Thomas or maybe Mr. McTavet?" I asked.

"It doesn't matter," Otto said, lifting his hand then realizing the bottle was gone.

"You do know the police are looking to question you," I said.

"I had nothing to do with it," he said.

"They're looking to pin this on Edward. They're going to grill you about all of the details of his life now and of his childhood and about why you're still a part of his life if he's really living an honest life," I said.

"I've got nothing to hide," he said.

"You're not listening to me," I said, leaning down to stare him right into the eyes. He had a little trouble focusing on me when I was that close, but he gave it an effort. "They aren't looking for the truth. They're not even looking for juicy secrets. They're looking for any reason at all they can pin this on him. And if you try to talk to them the way you are now, you're going to be giving them everything they want and more."

"I told you," he said, raising a wavering finger at me. "I told you they would."

"So why are you drinking then?" I asked.

His eyes filled with tears and I threw up my hands in surrender.

"I can't help him," he said, putting an arm over his eyes so we couldn't see him cry. "I can't do a thing for him."

"Not like this you can't," I said, but Sophie shot me a quelling look.

She might have sympathy for him, but I had none left.

"You're letting him down," I said.

"I know," he wailed.

Sophie nudged me back so she could take my place in front of Otto. She put her hands gently on his shoulders and waited for him to pull himself together and lower his arm.

"Otto," she said softly. "Why would Thomas be a target? Is he mixed up with something dangerous?"

"Not that I know of," Otto said. "But his father is a lawyer. A good one. He's managed to get a few of the worse sorts of gangsters put away despite the corruption in the police department and the courts. Someone might want to teach him a lesson by going after his boy."

"But no one here," I said. "Wait, is Thomas' father here?"

"No," Otto said. "I asked. He's at the governor's do. Pretty much anyone who isn't here is over there. More proper businessmen, though. Fewer gangsters."

"So his parents weren't even here?" Brianna said. "This really was a last-minute engagement, wasn't it? How strange it all is."

A door banged open on the other end of the kitchen and the sounds of dishes being washed promptly stopped.

"Wrong door," one of the waiters said. "The ballroom is down that way, and the powder room just down there."

"We're searching all the rooms," another man said. "We're looking for someone who seems to be hiding from us."

I looked to the others in alarm.

"Just let them take me," Otto said, struggling to his feet. I reached past Sophie to put a hand on his chest and gently shove him back down.

"Not like this," I said.

"You suggest we hide him until he sobers up?" Sophie asked, raising an eyebrow at me.

"I can fix it," Brianna said.

"You can fix it," Sophie said. "How?"

"I know a spell," she said, pulling out her wand.

"You can sober him up with a spell?" I asked.

"Yes," she said, raising her wand. Otto's eyes went wide, and he pressed back against the wall.

"How long have you known this spell?" Sophie asked.

"Since high school," Brianna said, her cheeks reddening. "It comes in handy at parties when someone drinks so much they become an ass."

"Sounds like just the thing," I said, looking down at Otto.

"Quick, then," Sophie said. Brianna whispered a few words then touched the tip of her wand to Otto's nose.

Otto blinked and just like that his eyes were clear and focused.

"Nice trick," Sophie said.

"I might have to have you come around more often," Otto said.

"Why don't you just try not drinking yourself into a stupor?" I asked.

"I didn't mean for *me*," Otto said.

"Come on, we have to get out of here," Sophie said. "We don't want to be in his company when they catch him, do we?"

"No, you don't," Otto said and bent over to pick up the bottle that still had a measure of champagne sloshing around within it.

"What are you doing?" I asked.

"Luring them into a false sense of not taking me seriously?" Otto said. "Go on. I'm fine."

There was a chaos of noise from the other side of the crates as the officers searched all of the cupboards and closets and the staff started shouting protests at the disarray.

Sophie then Brianna slipped back into the butler's pantry. I spared one last look back at Otto.

"Good luck," I said.

"Hey," he said just before I darted across. I looked back. "You promise to clear Edward's name if he's falsely accused?"

"Of course," I said.

"And mine?" he asked.

"Of course, Otto," I said.

"Thanks," he said, then waved me away.

The police officers' search had nearly worked its way across the kitchen. If I had waited a moment longer, it would have been too late. And from the look Sophie and Brianna gave me when I joined them in the butler's pantry, they knew it too.

We didn't look back, just walked across the butler's pantry like it was the more natural place in the world for us to be, back to the light of the party.

CHAPTER 11

*W*hen we slipped back into the ballroom, we found Coco looking around for us. She came over when she saw us, but her face was grim.

"What is it?" I asked.

"I found them," she said. "But I don't know how you're going to be able to talk to them. Edward is upstairs in what used to be one of my brothers' rooms."

"How is he? Did you get to talk to him?" I asked.

"No, I couldn't even see him, but I know he was in there. There are two men guarding his door, and they chased me away, but when I asked if it was Edward or Thomas in there, they said it was Edward."

"And Thomas?" Sophie asked.

"In my parents' room on the second floor," Coco said. "And also with two guards that wouldn't let me in there even when I said I had to fetch something for my mother."

"I thought your mother was in that room?" Brianna asked.

"No, she has a private sitting room that is next to it. That's where she is."

"Connecting?" I asked.

"There's a door from there to her closet and through that to her room," Coco said. "But there are police in the sitting room with her, so we can't get in that way either."

We all mulled this over.

"Is there anything you can do that doesn't involve talking to Edward or Thomas?" Coco asked.

I looked up at Brianna and Sophie. They gave me little nods.

"Yes," I said. "But we'd have to be alone to do it."

Coco's face brightened at once. "You can use my room," she said.

"What would really be helpful," Sophie said, "would be to see the balcony where everything happened."

"The police already searched it for clues," Coco said.

"So they won't be there now," Sophie said.

"We need to be alone there," Brianna said. "Alone and undisturbed."

"All right," Coco said. "I can help you do that."

"I can help, too," Charlotte said, and we all jumped. None of us had seen her approaching.

"What are you helping us with?" Sophie asked, trying to suss out how much Charlotte had overheard.

"You want to get upstairs, right?" Charlotte said. "Coco and I can distract the guard at the bottom of the steps. Then you can do... whatever."

I really wanted to get a look at the threads that ran through her form, to see if I could tell if she was trustworthy. I've blinked in and out of that other place before, but only in times where my fight or flight hormones were surging through me, when my power was jacked up to its highest setting. Trying to do it now, even if it worked, would probably involve me fainting or my eyes rolling back or any of a thousand other little things that would undermine our efforts to be unnoticed.

"How long can you keep the guard distracted?" Sophie asked.

"As long as you need," Charlotte said, but Coco looked less confident in that answer.

"How are you going to do it?" I asked. I had seldom met anyone easier to overlook completely than Charlotte. How could she possibly find a way to be more than a momentary distraction?

She gave me a disdainful look, then ran her hands through her hair and down over her clothes.

It was eerie. After she had shaken out the tight updo and made little adjustments to the neckline and waist of her dress, she went from the ultimate wallflower to something quite different. Not so much ravishing as recently ravished was my first thought, but then she threw the loose waves of hair out of her eyes and fixed her gaze on me.

The haughty anger was now something darkly flirtatious. Still haughty, but that somehow enhanced the flirty thing. I had no idea how she did that, or what it meant. I could well imagine the effect if she pinned that on one of the younger officers. The confusion as to her intent alone would be terribly, terribly distracting.

"That will work," Sophie said almost admiringly.

"Let's get upstairs then," I said, clutching my bag to make sure my wand was still concealed within it. Sophie and Brianna matched my gesture. Then we followed Charlotte and a clearly bemused Coco towards the doorway between the ballroom and the front hall.

"I'm afraid you all still have to stay inside," the young man at the door said. I recognized him from before, the one with the thick blond hair. But the fellow on the opposite side of the door was not McConnell. He was a shorter, darker fellow who looked, if anything, even younger. I supposed he was a rookie, but in truth, I would have taken him for not yet out of high school.

"That's Coco," the rookie said. "She's allowed to go where she wants."

The blond officer's eyes shifted to the spot in the middle of the hall, where the shape of a human body was still discernible under the cover of a pristine white tablecloth. "Of course, she can, but you really don't want to go this way, kid. Take the back stairs, yeah?"

Standing behind her I couldn't see her face, but Coco's shoulders slumped and then began to shake, and the sudden look of alarm on the faces of the two officers told me everything.

"Hey, kid," he said, reaching out a hand to comfort her then leaving it to hover uncertainly as if he wasn't sure if he was allowed. He looked desperately over at Charlotte.

"What's your name?" Charlotte asked him. He gave her a bare glance. Apparently, she wasn't doing the look yet.

"Larson," he said. I started at the name. I knew some Larsons in 2018: Nick Larson as well as his grandfather. Was there a resemblance between this man and them? Perhaps he was an ancestor?

Probably not. It was a terribly common name in this part of the world.

The Larson in question was getting more flustered by the minute with Coco's crying, and he looked imploringly to Charlotte. "Can't you take her somewhere and get her something?"

"She wants to say good-bye to her sister," Charlotte said.

"I don't know," he said. "I don't think that's a good idea. Or really my decision."

"Please," Charlotte said, putting an arm around the now loudly snuffling Coco.

I doubted Coco was acting. All she had needed to do was just let go of the iron control she had been exerting on her tears all evening.

"I should ask my boss," he said, but he didn't sound certain.

"Let the kid have a moment," the rookie said. "She won't disturb anything."

"I suppose not," Larson said.

"If you take her you can be sure she doesn't touch anything she's not supposed to," Charlotte said. "I'll stay here until she's done." Then, not waiting for an answer, she moved the sobbing Coco from her side to the officer's.

"All right," he relented. The near-panic on his face relaxed some-what when Coco stopped sobbing. He gave her a handkerchief, and she wiped her eyes with it then murmured something I couldn't catch. He nodded and, putting an arm around her, led her across the parquet floor. I could see she was all but dragging her feet, going as slowly as she could.

The rookie watched them go for a moment then turned. His eyes were almost on the three of us lingering too close to the doors, but before he could tell us to rejoin the others, Charlotte took a step closer to him and, judging from the sudden flush to his cheeks, hit him with that befuddling gaze.

"Come on," Sophie said, and slipped between the rookie's back and the doorframe, skirting the sides of the hall and jogging up the stairs. Charlotte had her hand on the rookie's arm, keeping him focused on her as Brianna and I followed Sophie.

The heels of our shoes rapped loudly off the wood floor, but Coco's renewed sobs were louder still and Larson had his hands full keeping her from collapsing on the floor at her sister's side. It was a heartrending sound, such pure hurt, and despair that I wanted to abandon everything and head back down the stairs to put my arms around Coco and give her every word of comfort I knew.

I had to remind myself that what Coco wanted more than anything was justice for her sister. I kept going up the stairs.

The second-floor balcony was silent, no sign of anyone up or down either of the corridors. We kept going up.

The light from the chandelier was indeed uncomfortably bright, and by the last few steps, I couldn't even really see where I was going. I kept a tight grip on the railing to be sure I didn't stumble.

"Now what?" Sophie asked as the three of us crouched at the top of the steps, as close as we could reckon to where Ivy had been standing. I was crouching with the light behind me, looking around for clues. But there was, of course, no blood here, no scuff marks on the floor-boards, nothing at all. I could see the outline of the little door that led to the playroom, and if I leaned forward I could see far enough down the hall to where two police officers sat on chairs outside the door to the room where they were keeping Edward, but nothing else.

Brianna and Sophie huddled closer to me, having also seen the officers. They hadn't looked our way, but if we made any sound at all they'd come to investigate, I was sure.

"I think I've worked out a spell," Brianna whispered.

"Then do it," Sophie whispered back.

"We three have to do it together," Brianna said. "Sophie, you use your senses like you usually do, and Amanda, do your sort of magic.

My spell will create a flow between the three of us, so we all see one picture made of both of those perceptions."

"You just figured this out now?" I asked.

"I've been thinking about it all night," Brianna said. "I'm not certain it will work, but I'd like to try. Even if it doesn't, you two will still see what you see."

"Let's try it," I said. Brianna held out her hands and Sophie and I each took one, then grabbed each other's hands to complete the circle. Then at Brianna's little nod, I closed my eyes, settling back on my heels and moving my awareness to the thread layer of the world.

For a moment I saw the threads all around me, but before I had the chance to start looking more closely at the knots and interlacings, I felt a surge of warmth flow from Brianna's hand into mine, through my body to my other hand and into Sophie. Then another wave passed through me in the other direction.

It was incredibly soothing, like taking a nap while floating on a lake, all warm and gently rocking on the waves.

I had the overwhelming urge to open my eyes.

When I did, I saw Brianna and Sophie also had their eyes open. I definitely felt more closely bonded with the two of them than I ever had before, but the spell didn't seem to be working for its intended effect.

Then I felt another wave of warmth wash over me from Sophie's direction, and I felt a rush of emotions all jumbled together: elation and joy and pride and nervousness and boredom and sadness, all crushed down under an indescribable fury.

I couldn't make sense of it and tried to summon back the threads. I didn't see them this time, but the emotions sort of ordered themselves into different places around the balcony, becoming distinct entities. Ivy's joy nearly overlapping with where I crouched, her father's elation and her mother's pride beside her. The nervousness seemed to be where I remembered Thomas standing. The sadness was down the corridor. Edward or Mary? I wasn't sure.

The anger I couldn't pinpoint. It was everywhere, and when I tried to focus on it, it grew stronger still. It was like a glass of dirty water knocked over a watercolor painting in progress, smearing and diluting and destroying all of the other colors.

Sophie's hand in mine tightened, and she made a small grunting noise of pain or effort or maybe both. I don't know what she did, but it was as if that glass righted itself and the other colors were restored.

But I still couldn't see where that anger was coming from. I squeezed both Brianna's and Sophie's hands and focused still harder on the threads I knew were there, just out of sight. Slowly, their forms started to develop like the outlines of a photograph in the pool of chemicals.

It was so hard. Why was this so hard? I concentrated harder, but I was making black dots burst across my vision appear more than I was bringing those threads into focus.

But there was a pattern in what threads I could see, a web that touched every glow of emotion on that balcony but focused most strongly on Ivy. But Ivy was where it was all flowing *to*. Where was it flowing *from*?

Suddenly there was a clatter of noise: someone running up the steps, falling, then getting up and running again. The picture that had almost been in focus was gone in a flash, and we all let go of each other's hands with a gasp.

"What happened?" Brianna asked. "What broke the spell?"

I looked to the top of the stairs to see Charlotte there. Her hands were on the top step as if she had crawled up the last bit of stairs after falling. Her hair and clothes were still in disarray, but now her eyes were wide with alarm. She had been about to crawl back down the steps but froze when my eyes met hers.

"Charlotte," I said, reaching out for her.

"What was that?" Charlotte demanded, her eyes growing wider still. "Who are you? *What* are you?"

"We can explain," Sophie said, but it was too late. Charlotte was running back down the stairs.

CHAPTER 12

 e scrambled to our feet and raced down the stairs. Coco and Larson were still standing together over Ivy's covered body, but they both looked up in alarm as we ran down the last few steps to the parquet floor of the hall.

"How did you get up there?" Larson asked, looking up the way we'd come then back over his shoulder at Ricci still standing in the doorway. Ricci shrugged, but after the officer turned back again his face darkened and I could see he was figuring it out.

"Where's Charlotte?" I asked Coco.

"I don't know," Coco said. "I thought she was…" she looked back at Ricci standing alone at the door.

"She just came downstairs. We were following her," I said.

"She didn't come down here," Coco said.

"Second floor," Sophie whispered, and we all three turned to go back up the stairs.

"Hold on," Larson said. "That area is off limits."

"Obviously we had permission to be up there since that's where we came from," I said. It always worked in the movies if you pretended like you belonged wherever you were trying to be. But I think it worked better if you had some sort of uniform to back up your story.

"They were supposed to be watching me," Coco said and sounded genuinely chagrined. "I gave them the slip so I could come see Ivy. But I suppose I better get back to my room before you tell my mother."

"Yes," I said.

"We'd be in more trouble than you, you know," Sophie said.

"I know. I'm sorry," Coco said and left Larson's side to come over to us.

But he didn't look like he was buying it.

"Ricci, watch the door. I'm going to escort them to Coco's room and make sure they stay there," he said.

That was less than ideal, but it was better than being in the ballroom. He waved for Coco to lead the way as he brought up the rear. Coco climbed the steps to the second floor then turned down the darkened corridor to the right.

As much as it had looked empty when we'd passed it before, there really were guards outside the master bedroom. But there was a little niche off the corridor, just deep enough for a pair of chairs and a large potted plant dying a slow, sunless death between them. One of the officers was sitting on a chair, but the other was pacing in front of the door. He raised an eyebrow as he saw the three of us following Coco, but relaxed when Larson came into view.

"This is mine," Coco said, opening a door at the very end of the hall.

"I'll be right out here," he said as we all passed into the room.

"Thank you," Coco said as if he were doing us a great service. Then she shut the door and waved for us to follow her past a little lounging area and then her canopied bed to the windows that overlooked the back garden.

"Did you find out anything?" she asked. Her eyes were red-rimmed from the crying, but she looked more at peace now, less crazed and tense from everything she was holding back.

"Not really," I said. "Someone up there was very angry, but we don't know who, and it still doesn't mean that this wasn't all an accident."

"But someone knocked me down," Coco said.

"I know," I said. "We haven't stopped looking. We're just running out of ways to look."

Coco's shoulders slumped. "If we don't give them someone else to blame, they're going to blame Edward. I already lost my sister. I don't think I can stand to see Edward..." She put a hand to her face, squeezing the bridge of her nose hard as if to stop the tears. "I wish there was a way I could help him."

"You are helping him," I said.

"You're helping us help him," Brianna said.

"If you're up for it, there is something else you can do for us," Sophie said.

"Anything," Coco said, her eyes brightening.

"We need to talk to Charlotte. She seemed pretty upset, and I think she's afraid of us," Sophie said.

"Why would she be afraid of you?" Coco asked.

"She saw something that looked strange. We just want to explain it to her," Sophie said.

"She knows all the hiding places that you know," I said.

"Not all of them," Coco said.

"You're the perfect person to find her," I said.

"Probably the only person who could," Sophie said. "If you can get past the guard at the door."

"That won't be a problem," Coco said and turned to pull her night-stand away from the wall, revealing the outline of another little door. "But what are you going to be doing while I look for Charlotte?"

"We have to discuss some things with each other," Sophie said. "Compare impressions."

"List what clues we have and our theories and what we'll do next," I said.

Coco nodded. "If it helps, there's a chalkboard just over there in my old play area. I haven't used it in years, but there's still chalk in the tray."

"Thanks," I said.

"When you find Charlotte, bring her back here at once," Sophie said. "It's important."

Coco nodded then stooped to crawl inside the little door.

"It might be too late," Brianna said, biting her lip. "She was terrified. And if it isn't witches she thinks we are, it's surely something worse."

"But who would she tell?" I asked.

"Mary? Or Ricci now that she's friendly with him?" Sophie said.

"And would they believe her?" I asked.

"We just have to hope that Coco gets to her first," Sophie said.

"But I wonder how much she saw of what we were doing?" Brianna said. "Without a gift for magic, she should only have been able to see the three of us holding hands."

"Well," Sophie said. "Maybe more than that."

"Like what?" I asked.

"Well, you were sitting sort of three-quarters turned away from her, so I don't know how much she saw of your face, but it was…"

"Scary," Brianna said.

"Scary?" I said.

"You were doing that thing you do when the power hits you," Sophie said. "Hair floating, eyes glowing with this electric fire."

"And you were floating," Brianna said. "Just a bit."

"Wow," I said. "I hadn't felt any of that. I hadn't even felt particularly powerful. It felt like I couldn't even summon my own magic. I was trying so hard, but it wasn't coming."

"Oh yes, it was," Sophie said, and Brianna nodded.

"What do you mean?" I asked.

Sophie looked at Brianna then held out her hands, palms up. One looked perfectly ordinary, the one that had been holding Brianna's hand.

The other was bright red as if she had tried to take a hot pan off the stove without using any sort of mitt.

Brianna held out her hands and the hand of hers I had been holding looked if anything, worse.

"I'm so sorry," I said.

"Your power is strange," Brianna said. "I wished I understood it better. It's like you have infinite amounts, and yet so little control."

"I'm sorry," I said again.

"No, I didn't mean it like that, like it's your fault," Brianna said. "I meant control like…" She looked to Sophie for help.

"Like too much raging water trying to pass through a very tight space," Sophie said. "The more you try to control it, the more you increase the pressure on that water. I don't think you can make it… less."

I looked down at my own unmarred palms.

"Should we try the spell again?" Brianna asked. "It will be trickier at a distance, but we could still try."

"No, I don't think we'll bring that anger into focus," I said.

"It didn't feel magic, at least," Sophie said. "Maybe that's why we're having so much trouble with it. For once, our murderer isn't a magical person or an ordinary person using a magic artifact. We might not be equipped for this."

"Maybe," I said, but I wasn't convinced. There had to be something we could do. We were witches.

"Maybe we couldn't focus it because it was coming from multiple people," Brianna said.

"So now we're going with conspiracy?" Sophie asked.

"No, the flow was going the other way," I said. At their confused looks, I added, "I think it had one hidden source, but it was flowing so strongly towards so many other targets, we couldn't pinpoint it."

"We searched for signs of magic before we came into the house, and we all agreed there weren't any," Brianna said. "But what if we did that sort of search again, not for a magical person, but just for any person with ill intent?"

I barked out a laugh, and they both shot me an alarmed look. "Sorry. It's just that, Otto already told us that a ton of the partygoers are gangsters or guys working both sides of the law. I think we're going to be drowning in ill intent."

"Malevolence, then," Sophie said. "That was the overwhelming feeling I was getting."

"I got anger," Brianna said.

"Me too," I said. "But whoever or whatever was angry, that was a malevolent being."

"I agree," Sophie said. "This wasn't a normal person driven to murder. This was a person who was mad at the whole world and took it out on Ivy."

"Okay," Brianna said. "Let's try looking for that. A dark heart, I guess."

"A dark heart," Sophie and I agreed.

We sat down on the rug in front of the fireplace that was just barely glowing with the light from a banked fire. Then we took hands and closed our eyes.

Nothing happened.

"Amanda," Sophie said. "You have to do this."

"I'm doing it," I said.

"No, she's right. You're holding back," Brianna said.

"I don't want to hurt you again," I said.

"You won't," Sophie said, but then hedged. "Maybe don't try so hard to bring anything vague into focus. Let's just see what a casual look around shows us."

"Okay," I said and squeezed their hands. "I can do that."

I glimpsed the world of threads for only a fraction of a second this time before the waves of warmth started rolling between us. Then I watched with half-opened eyes as I began to picture the home around us.

It was like watercolor dots of emotions again. Or maybe more like blots, the edges undefined, flowing like the painter had made a second pass of the brush with too much water. Or like a wind was blowing through them, disrupting their outlines.

But I could tell they were people even without seeing the pattern of the threads. I could sense a blot that was swirling with so many different colors fighting for dominance, a blot that was moving with determination from room to room at the back of the house on the first floor.

Coco. Coco on a quest to find Charlotte, letting her drive to complete that quest push all of her other feelings to the back of her mind. But they were still there, roiling away.

I turned my attention away from Coco and spread my awareness over the entire house, then floated it up from floor to floor.

So many blots of color. So many minds processing so many emotions.

I lingered the longest on the blot I saved for last: the one that was Edward. I watched the colors swirl around inside him, the way the invisible wind or brush of water moved through it, pulling bits away in tendrils that tapered off to nothing. I didn't know what it meant, this thing that I was seeing. I expected it was part of Sophie's way of seeing patterns.

But the colors spoke to me. I could feel his confusion and sadness and fear.

And loneliness. More than anything else, he was feeling alone.

I wished there was some way I could disrupt those feelings, to replace them with a feeling of another, warmer color. He was surrounded by people who cared about him. Otto and we three, but also Coco and even Coco and Ivy's father. Their regard and worry for him was real. I could see those watercolor tendrils that tapered off their own blots pointing his way. If I saw just threads and not colors I was sure they were all connected.

But Edward couldn't see it. And he wasn't feeling it.

Brianna and Sophie squeezed my hands, and at that signal, I opened my eyes. I blinked the visions away. When we finally took a real look at each other, we all shook our heads at once.

"Nothing," Sophie said. "I didn't feel a single person with anything like that anger inside of them."

"Nor I," I said.

"I didn't even sense where Charlotte was," Brianna sighed. "And we know she's still in the house. Are we doing this correctly?"

But none of us had an answer to that question.

"Have we run out of things to try?" Sophie asked.

"No," I said. "I want to talk to Edward."

CHAPTER 13

I started to get up and head towards the door, but Sophie caught my wrist.

"Wait, let's talk this through," she said.

"We've left him alone long enough," I said. "He's so isolated and despairing. We can't leave him like that a moment longer."

"I think you're projecting," Sophie said.

"What are you talking about? We just felt everything he was feeling," I said.

"I didn't," Sophie said. "I knew he was on the third floor. I sensed that. But as to the rest?" She looked over at Brianna, who shrugged and then shook her head.

I sank back down to the floor. "We were all seeing the same thing, right?"

"A projection of the house like a dollhouse with blots of color inside," Brianna said.

"I didn't see the dollhouse," I said. "I guess I was just in it. But the blots of color were people."

"Yes," Brianna agreed.

"I saw the dollhouse," Sophie said, "but my colors were more like streaks in a stream. Moving, like dancing, but never quite fading away."

"So we created a thing together, but we all have different perceptions of it," I said. "Didn't you two see Edward?"

"I sensed him upstairs, where we already knew he was," Brianna said. "I was worried about who Charlotte might be talking to, so I tried to focus on Coco and her. But Coco hasn't found her yet, and I couldn't sense Charlotte anywhere."

"I didn't either, but I wasn't trying too," Sophie said.

"Nor I," I said, but turned to Sophie. "What were you trying to sense?"

"I was focused on the library," Sophie said. "I thought perhaps a malevolent heart would either be one of them, or in their custody, or just as interested in what the police were up to as we are."

"But you didn't find anything?" I asked.

"No," she said. "Otto is still being questioned. He was in some discomfort. I'm not sure they are being kind with their questions."

"Great," I said. "Another thing we have to stop. The police are botching this. We really have to step in."

"And do what?" Brianna asked. "Declare ourselves witches and command everyone to obey us?"

"Obviously not," I said.

"Then what?" she asked.

"I don't think Otto would want us to intervene," Sophie said. "He knew what he was up against when he let them take him into the library. I don't think it's gone outside the realm of things he was prepared to face."

"All right," I said. "But I'm still going upstairs to see Edward. And no one is going to stop me."

"How are you going to get past our guard?" Sophie asked.

"Through there," I said, pointing at Coco's little secret door.

"It's going to be tight," she said, swinging the door open to look inside. "And dusty."

"Well, it's not like I was ever going to wear this dress again anyway," I said. But even so, I gathered the long skirt up around my waist and tied it up so I wouldn't trip on it while I was crawling.

The crawl space smelled like old dust and mouse droppings, and it was bone-chillingly cold. By the time I reached the far door which opened out onto a shadowed corner of the back stairs landing my hands were numb, and I had an angry red scrape down the side of one knee from when I'd brushed up against a protruding nail.

When Sophie and Brianna were out of the door we all three headed up the stairs to the third floor.

The guards that had been distantly visible from the top of the main staircase were only a few feet away from us here. I quickly ducked back behind the corner, and we crept back down to the second-floor landing.

"There's still two of them," I said.

"Awake?" Sophie asked.

"Very alert," I said. "They nearly saw me."

"I can try being flirty," Sophie said. "It worked for Charlotte with Ricci."

"These are older guys," I said. "Maybe not immune to your charms, but better trained at being professional when on the job. I don't think we're going to be able to talk our way past them or even distract them long enough for me to slip by."

"I have a sleeping spell," Brianna said, and Sophie and I both started to perk up. But her face was glum. "It's not great, though. It comes out of my wand like sand and takes a moment to work. I'm not sure I can get close enough, or get it in their eyes, or not get nabbed before it has a chance to work."

"Maybe we should find Coco," I said. "If Edward is in one of her brothers' rooms, there must be a passage that leads there as well."

"Wait," Sophie said. "Let's go back to Brianna's plan."

"No, getting Coco is a better plan," Brianna said. "Mine's bad. Not doable."

"Maybe not for you alone," Sophie said. "But I think together we can make it work."

"One of your breezes?" I guessed. She nodded. "Can you do one strong enough to carry sand?"

"I guess we'll see," she said. "I'm going to the top of the stairs. Once I get moving, Brianna, you toss up that magic sand from your wand. Then we'll see."

"And if it doesn't work, they'll see you," I said.

"Then you two run for it and figure something out without me," Sophie said. "Ready?"

Brianna took out her wand and gave it a little flick then nodded.

Sophie slipped off her shoes and handed them to me before creeping back up the stairs. Then she began to dance. This was nothing like her dancing at the party earlier. I could feel the power flowing around her as she enticed the very air around her to dance with her in ever more powerful waves that I could almost see.

There was a murmur of male voices, one of the guards speaking to the other one. Sophie kept on dancing, building momentum.

"Miss? You're meant to be downstairs," one of them said, and I could hear his footsteps as he got up from this chair and came down the corridor towards Sophie.

"Now," Sophie called to us.

Brianna spoke a word and made a gesture with her wand like a fly fisher casting off. Golden grains showered out of the end of her wand, falling at once towards the floorboards.

But Sophie's wind snatched most of them up, whirling around her body once then moving in a wavering line like a gymnast's dancing ribbon down the corridor.

Sophie stopped dancing, her arms wrapping around her body as she came to a halt. She rose up on tiptoe, peering down the dark corridor. Then her face lit up.

"It worked!" she said.

"But for how long?" I asked as Brianna, and I joined her on the landing.

"I've only ever seen it used on children," Brianna said. "I don't know how long it will last on a grown man, but I would think it would be something short of all night."

"That's a little bit open-ended, don't you think?" I asked, handing Sophie her shoes.

"I'll stay here as lookout," Sophie said. "In case anyone comes up the stairs."

"I'll be lookout outside the bedroom door," Brianna said, and the two of us went down the corridor to where the two police officers were slumped on their chairs, snoring loudly.

"I guess we'll know if they start to wake up," I said.

"I can dose them again if they start to stir," Brianna said. "Take all the time you need."

"Thanks," I said. I grasped the doorknob, but it wouldn't turn. "Locked."

"Oh," Brianna said, looking down at the guards. "Maybe one of them has the key in his pocket."

"No worries," I said, catching her arm before she could start pawing through their clothing. "Let them sleep. I have a workaround."

She raised one eyebrow in question, then both when she saw the golden key I pulled from my beaded bag.

"You brought that with?" Brianna asked. "To a party?"

"So far it's been more useful than my wand," I said and slipped it inside the keyhole. It turned with a soft click, and the door was open.

"Don't forget why we're here," she said as I put the key away.

"To solve a murder," I said. "But also to comfort a friend."

"One is more time-sensitive than the other," Brianna said.

"Is it?" I asked. Then I slipped through the door, shutting it behind me before she could respond.

CHAPTER 14

I regretted closing the door when I found the room in total darkness, the only light from two windows set low to the floor under gables. They overlooked the back garden, but the lights around the patio were too far away to provide more than a dim glow, and the night sky was overcast.

"Edward?" I whispered, brushing my hand over the wall beside the door in a futile search for a light switch.

"Amanda?" He didn't sound like he believed it was really me. I tried to follow the sound of his voice but tripped over a chair that lurked in the darkness. "Is it you?" he asked.

"Hold on," I said and pulled my traitorous wand out of my beaded bag. Making light was one of the few bits of magic we had mastered together, but we had failed at it just hours before. My only real hope was that it would work better when the need was real.

I had never been a particularly good test taker, after all.

I summoned power and directed it to flow into the wand, gritting my teeth against the nausea that rose up in my stomach. It still felt so wrong, so not a part of me.

But we managed a glowing ball of light that drifted slowly out of the end of the wand to rest softly on the floor.

"What is that?" Edward asked. I could see him now. I told myself that his features looked pale and thin because of the unfriendly light, but I didn't really manage to convince myself. He looked like someone who had been distraught for more than the course of an afternoon and evening.

Then a rise of anger burned away the last lingering effects of nausea from working with my wand. They had cuffed him to the foot of the heavy iron bedstead. The door was locked, with two guards, and yet they had cuffed him in a way where he couldn't even scratch his own face if he needed to. He couldn't even sit upright. He was sort of lurched to one side. I could imagine how stiff he was, how much it was going to both hurt and yet be a relief when he could stand again.

"This is lunacy," I said, dropping to my knees beside him and examining the lock on his cuffs. "Who had these manacles just in the house?"

"How did you get in here? There are guards outside," Edward said.

"I have ways," I said, taking the golden key back out of my bag. It looked too big to fit into the lock on the cuffs, but when I tried it, I found the very tip could slide in. Because of course it could. There was a click, and the manacles fell from his wrists to the floor.

"How did you get the key?" he asked, sitting up straight and stretching his arms with a groan.

"I have a key of my own," I said, stuffing it and my wand back in my bag.

He raised an eyebrow at the sight of my wand but said nothing.

"Edward, I need to know what happened," I said. "Otto is in the library with the chief and the detectives. He's stalling the questioning, I'm certain of it. But they will be talking to you and Thomas when they are done with him. We don't have much time."

"What happened?" he said as if he didn't understand the question.

"Edward, the police are trying to pin this on you," I said, leaning in to force him to focus on my eyes, to see I was deadly serious. "It had to be either you or Thomas, and Thomas' family are important. If nothing can be proved otherwise, you will be found guilty."

"But Thomas didn't do it either," Edward said, then paused. "I don't think."

"Coco thought there was..." but then I stopped myself. "Never mind. Tell me first what you saw. You were upstairs the entire time, weren't you? You're the one Thomas kept looking to?"

"Yes," he admitted, dropping his eyes to examine the chaff marks from the manacles, barely visible in the yellowish light from my magic globe. "Where do you want me to start?"

"Mr. McTavet gathered everyone to hear the announcement," I said.

"Yes," he said and took a breath. "Mr. McTavet and I had been in his study just before. Talking. Mrs. McTavet came in and said it was time, and Mr. McTavet asked me to go up with him. I would rather just have left, frankly. But he's still one of my bosses at the bank, and none of what happened was his fault. Quite the opposite. So I went up. But I didn't want to go out on that balcony. I suppose it would have been gracious to do so, but I wasn't feeling particularly gracious."

"Thomas was signaling you to join them?" I asked.

"Yes," he said.

"Why?"

"To show there were no hard feelings, I suppose," he said.

I desperately wanted to ask if there were hard feelings, but I had to stay focused on proving his innocence. Talking about feelings was sure to explode into a huge conversation we didn't have time for. Even if I really wanted to know.

"But I just couldn't," Edward said with a shrug.

"Coco and Charlotte were also there," I said.

"Were they?" he asked, his gaze shifting up and to the right as he thought back. "Yes, they were there. But not near the balcony. Closer to the wall. They were well clear of the scuffle."

"There was a scuffle," I said, my heart sinking.

"To my everlasting regret," Edward said, not looking at me.

"What happened?"

"After Mr. McTavet sent everyone back into the ballroom, he turned to speak to his wife. I don't know what about. He wasn't pleased with the turn of events, but his wife was. I think he was annoyed with her about that. He wasn't inclined to celebrate as much as she wanted him too.

"At any rate, now that the attention of the crowd had shifted away, I decided to speak to Ivy. We hadn't had a moment alone since she told me she had chosen Thomas over me. Her mother had been with her in that moment, and then her father and Thomas as well. And Coco and Mary and Charlotte. I hadn't had a single chance to say a word to her at all."

"You were angry?" I asked.

"Angry? No!" Edward said. "I mean, it was a shock at first. I don't imagine anyone is jilted and doesn't feel a lot of terrible things. But I was never angry. All I wanted was a moment to tell her I wished her and Thomas well. But when I approached her to say so, I guess Thomas took that wrong. I'm not sure why. It's not like I was rushing forward with my blood hot or anything. I had my hand extended to shake hers and his as well."

"So Thomas started the fight?"

"It wasn't really a fight," he said. "It was far too awkward to call it that. I had my hand out to shake, and Thomas I guess wanted to knock it aside, to step between Ivy and me. But he sort of tripped and fell into me. I grabbed his shoulder to help him steady his balance. But it must have looked like something else to Ivy because she threw herself on Thomas' back as if to pull him off of me. Thomas pulled away from me, but too violently, and fell back against Ivy."

"And that's when she went over the railing?" I asked.

"No, she only fell against it," he said.

"Are you sure?"

He considered for a moment. "Yes. She only fell against it. But she cried out. Not loud, just a little sound of pain, but it made Thomas' blood boil. He swung at me." Edward touched a spot over his eye. I leaned forward to see more clearly, gently brushing back the locks of hair that had fallen over his forehead.

There had been blood, smeared away at some point but leaving little streaks to stain his skin. The goose egg underneath was mostly concealed by his eyebrow, but visible now that I knew to look for it.

"He struck you," I said.

"It was a trying day for all of us," Edward said.

"Why do you excuse him?" I asked.

"How can I not?" he asked. "I know what he is feeling now. We both lost a fiancée today. We're both wondering how much we are to blame."

"Did you hit him back?" I asked.

"No," he said. "But who knows what I might have done if the next moment had not occurred."

"This is when Ivy really did fall?"

"Yes. Thomas had just struck me, and I was seeing stars. Then there was blood in my eyes. I couldn't see what happened, but I heard Ivy scream. The way the echo of her voice through the hall changed as she fell. The way she…"

He didn't finish, but I knew what he meant. The sound of her body hitting the floor.

"So you don't know for sure, but Thomas had opportunity. He was closest to her," I said.

"There wasn't time," Edward said. "From punching me to turn and push her? No, there wasn't enough time."

"Are you absolutely sure?" I asked. "Time can run differently in such moments. An eyeblink can be an eternity. Or vice versa."

"I concede my perception of time might be off," Edward said. "I felt the world wanting to slip away from me for a moment. I think I was about to pass out. Thomas does box at a club in the city."

"There you are," I said.

"But no," he said. "I don't believe it of him. He was only striking me in the first place because Ivy was jostled into the railing and cried out as if hurt. He was protecting her, misguided as that impulse was. To turn from that to murder her? No."

"Was anyone close enough to Ivy then to push her besides Thomas?" I asked.

Edward touched his fingertips to his forehead and flinched. "Not that I could see. But Amanda, I couldn't see. You can't condemn him on so little."

"I'm not trying to condemn him. I'm trying to exonerate you," I said.

"Thank you," he said. "I don't even know how you're here. It's like I summoned you with a wish."

My stomach flipped over at that, but I told it to hold still. This was not the time.

"Coco invited the three of us, I guess when she still thought this was going to be your engagement party too," I said.

"I'm not surprised," he said. "She knew I didn't have any family to stand with me."

"She loved you like a brother already," I said. "She still does. She is also part of the reason I'm here now in this room with you. She knows you're not the guilty party and she won't stand to see injustice done. She's helping the three of us and Otto to clear your name."

"But if it wasn't me or Thomas, who was it?" he asked.

"I'm working on that," I said. The little globe of light on the floor was starting to sputter and die, but I couldn't complain. As unpleasant as its illumination had been, it had lasted far longer than I had expected. "Coco insists that someone knocked her down. So you were both trying to recover from a blow the moment Ivy fell."

"Who knocked her down?" he asked. "Did I bump into her when I fell back?"

"No," I said. "She thinks someone else was up there with you all."

He frowned. "I don't think so. But even before Thomas punched me, it was hard to see up there."

"Yes, that's a common theme so far," I said. I poked at the globe, and it shot up a couple of sparks like a pathetic volcano then lapsed further towards darkness.

"What is that thing?" Edward asked.

"I'll explain later," I said. "Just now I have to talk to Thomas."

"I understand," he said. "I wish you could stay, but I understand."

I raised a foot to stomp on the last of the light but hesitated. "Did you want me to reshackle you? It might be hard to explain how you freed yourself, but on the other hand, you looked very uncomfortable."

"I was," he said. "I don't care what they think. Leave me free." He wrapped his arms around himself, turning towards the wall as if to try to sleep.

The ache in my heart was almost more than I could bear. I wanted to sit down beside him, to put my arms around him and stay with him in the darkness.

But I couldn't. And not just because I had to go speak to Thomas, and to follow up every other lead I could find to prove him innocent.

I couldn't because the least kind thing I could possibly do for him in this moment, on this day when all of his hopes were so cruelly crushed, would be to make him believe he might have a different future with me. We had no future.

I really hated my life.

"Don't despair," I said. "You may have no family in the world just now, but you have many friends. Loyal, loving friends who will not rest until you are out of harm's way. Edward, you are not alone."

"Thank you," he said. He didn't look back at me, but his words were brighter than any he had spoken since I had come into the room.

I stomped out the light and left him in the darkness.

CHAPTER 15

$\mathcal{I}$ locked the door again behind me then looked up at Brianna. She gave a little wave for me to follow her back down the hall to where Sophie was standing at the top of the stairs. Brianna motioned for Sophie to start dancing up another wind, then summoned a spray of obsidian-like sand from the end of her wand. Sophie sent it flying down the hall to the two guards still snoring away in the chairs.

They both woke with a loud snort, and we quickly raced down the stairs, all of the way back to the darkened corridor behind the ballroom.

"What did he say?" Brianna asked me, but there were a group of men talking together just a few feet away in the corridor, and I shook my head.

"Not here," I said. We continued down the corridor to the bright lights of the ballroom. A crowd of angry partygoers was gathered at the far set of doors, demanding that the police let them leave the house.

"Oh dear," a woman near us said. "I do hope there isn't a fight."

I slowly turned as I looked around the room for any sign of Otto or Coco or Charlotte, but they were nowhere to be seen.

"It's too crowded to talk here either," I said. Even as I said it, something bumped me hard enough to send me staggering back half a step until Brianna caught me.

"Parlor," Sophie said, and we followed her to find that room fortunately empty, although someone had left out a tea service on one of the tables. Brianna tapped the pot with her wand to warm it up then poured out cups for each of us.

Once we were sitting in front of the fireplace, our chairs drawn as closely together as we could move them, I told them everything that had passed between Edward and me.

Well, mostly everything.

"So he doesn't think Thomas is guilty either," Sophie said, stirring her tea over and over with a little spoon. "That complicates things."

"We aren't looking to blame Thomas, though," Brianna said. "We're looking for the real culprit. Aren't we?"

"Yes," Sophie sighed, setting her spoon aside but not touching her tea. "I'm just saying, if Thomas were guilty, it would be easier to prove than it will be for us now to find this mysterious extra person up on the balcony that no one got a good look at."

"Maybe Mr. or Mrs. McTavet saw something?" Brianna asked hopefully.

"If they had, I'm sure the police would know it already," I said. "They'd be looking for someone who isn't Thomas or Edward. But they haven't. They are only building the case against Edward, not searching for a different suspect."

"Maybe if we went back up to the third floor and tried that spell again?" Brianna said.

"I don't think it will help," Sophie said.

"Besides, everything we've done so far we've gotten away with, but the police are getting suspicious. The guards outside Edward's room know something happened. They'll be more alert now. And they might hear us on the balcony now that they'll be more vigilant," I said.

"So what do we do?" Sophie asked.

"Talk to Thomas," I said. "There is nothing else."

"But Edward doesn't think he did it," Brianna said.

"Edward is kind to a fault," I said. "To a fault. He doesn't want to believe that Thomas might do it."

"I wish we had known Thomas before," Brianna said. "We have no real sense of his character."

"He had means and opportunity," I said. "He had knocked Ivy back into the railing once before."

"By mistake," Brianna said.

"And he was still the one closest to her when she fell," I went on.

"And as to motive?" Sophie asked.

"Maybe it was an accident," Brianna said.

"No," I said. "Well, maybe. But consider this. We already know he trains as a boxer. His reflexes are faster than his thinking, right?"

"Can we assume that?" Sophie asked, but I ignored her.

"He overreacted to Edward trying to speak to Ivy," I said. "Then he overreacted even more to Ivy getting bumped against the railing. It's very doubtful she was even hurt then, and besides that, it would've been more Thomas' fault than Edward's."

"So?" Sophie asked.

"I'm establishing a pattern of behavior," I said. "Clearly Thomas Weingarten is a man not in control of his own temper. We know there was this extreme, unprovoked escalation in a very short period of time. Is taking it one step further so inconceivable?"

"Yes!" someone cried from the doorway, and we all jumped to realize that at some point on our conversation we had neglected to keep our voices down.

"Mary!" Brianna said, for indeed that was who had overheard us.

She looked a mess, eyes red and blotchy, a coffee stain on the skirt of her gown. But I quickly realized that her body shook not with grief but with anger.

"How dare you?" she demanded, looking straight at me.

"What have I done?" I asked.

"Accuse Thomas. What proof do you have of what you say?" she asked, hands curling into fists.

Sophie leaped to her feet and pulled Mary into the room to sit in the chair she had just vacated. She made little murmuring sounds and comforting gestures, but Mary would not take the hint to be quieter.

"I wasn't accusing him," I said. "We were just discussing theories."

"You sounded like you were sure," Mary said. "You sounded like you were ready to hang him."

"I'm not sure of anything," I said. "I haven't even had a chance to speak with him."

"Why would you speak with him?" Mary asked. "You sound like you think you're the one investigating Ivy's murder and not the police."

"The police have sealed themselves off in the library to question all the wrong people," I said, crossing my arms. "Someone has to actually investigate."

"You're not trying to solve her murder, you're trying to absolve your friend," Mary said. "At the expense of my own."

"We're not," Sophie said, the only one of the three of us still capable of keeping her voice down, save Brianna who had fallen silent the moment the angry talking had started.

I took a deep breath, then three more. I forced my arms to unfold, although they felt like dead weights now hanging at my sides. "Edward didn't do it. And he told me he didn't believe Thomas did either," I said.

"When did you speak to Edward?" she asked.

"A moment ago," I said.

"How?"

"The usual way," I said, then plowed on before she could ask another probing question. "Coco also said there was a stranger up on the balcony with you all. Are you sure you didn't see anything more? Anything that would clear all this up?"

"No," Mary said, her voice thick. "I wished I had. I wished I could clear all this up. But you must believe me that Thomas would never do this. He isn't capable of it."

"Physically, he is," I said.

"Physically, any of us are," Sophie said, and I had to admit that was true. Ivy had been petite. Coco at thirteen was already taller than her sister and with quite a bit more heft.

"I was referring to his moral character," Mary said.

"Well, I don't know him," I admitted.

"I know you don't. If you did, you'd never be able to suggest the things you were suggesting. His father is a lawyer renowned across the Midwest for his high ethical standards. Thomas is cut from the same cloth. He's had the most refined of upbringings, has always been the model his peers were meant to emulate. He simply could not do this."

"Lucky for you the police agree," I said darkly. "Which is why Edward has to be their scapegoat. Edward who has no prominent family name, no renowned father or refined upbringing. The fact that he, also, could never do this is never going to enter anyone's mind."

"I wasn't saying that," Mary said.

"Weren't you?" I shot back.

"Amanda, you know she wasn't," Sophie said. "Please, take a moment to center yourself. You're not thinking clearly."

"Neither is she," I said. Although I was pretty aware that I sounded like a sullen, moody preteen in that moment.

"No, I am not," Mary admitted. "I can't. Not when it comes to... this."

"Thomas," I said. "You can't think clearly when it comes to Thomas."

Mary looked down at the mangled mess of a handkerchief clutched in her hand.

"You were upset before any of this happened," I said. "The engagement announcement was a shock to you. You ran away. No, not away. You ran upstairs. To demand answers."

"I wasn't going to demand anything," she said, but her hand around the handkerchief was forming a fist again.

"Surely someone owed you an explanation," I said. "Your best friend changes her mind so drastically, so dramatically, and she doesn't even tell you ahead of time. She must have had opportunity. Was she just being cruel?"

"Amanda, what are you talking about?" Brianna asked.

"Charlotte and I arrived later than we intended," Mary said. "Ivy and Mrs. McTavet were both glowing with happiness, but servants were constantly interrupting to ask questions about the food or the band or a thousand other things. I guess she didn't have the time."

"Didn't she?" I asked.

Mary tried to sniff back a fresh wave of tears.

"She could've made the time," I said. "She should have."

"Yes," Mary said, crying in earnest now. "She should have. She was my best friend. I was here for her, but she didn't even think of me."

"Did she know?" I asked. "How you felt about Thomas?"

"I never said it explicitly," Mary said, her voice barely audible. Sophie slid an arm around her, and Mary rested her head gratefully on Sophie's shoulder.

"She was your best friend," I said. "She knew."

"Yes," Mary said. "I think she did."

"Hold on," Brianna said, fingers fluttering as if she were adding up all the little clues. "Oh! Mary was in love with Thomas."

"Not was," Mary said miserably. "Am. Always have been, and heaven help me always will be."

"He's not worthy of you," I said.

"No, he never played me false," Mary insisted. "I always knew how he felt about Ivy. He's loved her since we were kids. But she didn't want him. But he liked me well enough. And I knew that as soon as Ivy was settled with another, then his heart would finally be free."

"I'm still not liking him," I said. "Charlotte doesn't either, does she?"

"Charlotte," Mary said, then seemed to swallow back her first attempt at completely that thought. She took a breath and spoke with more calm. "Charlotte is difficult. She always has been even as a baby. There's no accounting for her moods. And if she takes a disliking to someone, nothing will ever change that."

"Did Thomas do something to her years ago then?"

"If he had, it was some trifling little thing that she'll never let go of," Mary said. "Please, just speak with Thomas as you spoke with Edward and then speak to me as to his character. Please."

"That's reasonable," Sophie said, looking up at me.

"Quite," I said. "And what we were going to do next anyway."

"Oh, thank goodness," Brianna said. "For a minute there I thought you were going to argue that Mary was the murderer."

"She had motive," I said.

"Amanda!" Sophie chided.

"But not opportunity," I went on. "She was too far away. Every witness agrees on that."

Sophie was still staring daggers at me, but Mary took no offense.

"You'll think better of Thomas after you speak with him," Mary said. "But please, don't mention me. I don't really enter into things."

"You never told him how you felt either?" Sophie asked.

"Heavens, no!" Mary gasped.

"If you had entered into things more, perhaps this whole day would have ended very differently," I said.

"Amanda! You can't possibly put that blame on Mary!" Sophie said.

"No, I wasn't blaming Mary," I said. "It's just I'm finding it all a bit ironic. We're working so hard to catch her killer, and yet with every fresh detail I learn about Ivy, I like her less."

"We aren't doing this for her," Brianna said.

"No, we're not," I agreed. Then I pushed myself up from my chair and tipped my head back, trying to judge from what I remembered from our spell before where Thomas would be now in relation to where we were. Almost directly overhead, I decided.

And I immediately knew how right I was when I saw him fall headfirst past the window.

CHAPTER 16

I don't know how I knew it was Thomas, having only glimpsed a figure dressed like almost every man in atten-dance at the party. He fell past the window in the blink of an eye, but I was absolutely certain it was him.

And, to judge by the sudden sobbing scream, so was Mary.

I ran to the window and unlocked it. It opened out like a French door, although too tall to step through. I had to sit on the pane and swing my legs over before I could drop down into the snow and run to the crumpled form a few feet away.

Yeah, the dress was totally ruined now.

He had fallen into a bank where the snow that had been shoveled off the patio had piled up. At first, I wasn't even certain if he'd been hurt. He had only been on the second floor, after all, and the snow was deep.

But he wasn't moving, and when I came close enough to kneel beside him, it was clear he wasn't breathing.

He had landed in the deep snow, but head first. I was certain his neck had snapped at once. It would have been quick.

I hoped.

I looked up and could just make out the outlines of a balcony above. He hadn't fallen from a window then; the master bedroom had its own little veranda overlooking the garden. The light that so dimly illuminated the room Edward was in on the third floor did little more for the second floor. I saw nothing.

But I kept looking up anyway. Was someone there? Someone who knew the poor light so much closer to me than to them was preventing me from seeing them?

"Amanda?" Brianna called from the window. "Is it Thomas? Is he all right?"

I didn't look her way or down at Thomas. I just waited.

And sure enough, a shadow moved. Someone had been there, looking down at me.

They were getting away.

"Amanda!" Brianna called as I raced towards the house. I saw her out of the corner of my eye crawling out the window, but I didn't wait. I found a trellis covered with dried vines and a dusting of snow and saw that it ended just under a window on the second floor. I flung off my shoes, useless for climbing with their slick bottoms, and pulled myself up the surprisingly sturdy wood.

"Thomas!" Mary was crying, her voice now also outside in the garden. I focused on the window that was my goal. It too opened out like French windows, but fortunately had been left unlocked. It still took a bit of work to get it to open from the outside.

Good thing I'm not the type to be vain about my nails. They were a bloody mess by the time I had the window open wide enough to climb inside the house.

The master bedroom was almost ridiculously spacious, with two enormous beds as well as two separate sitting areas and a variety of doors. They must have separate closets and bathrooms and even separate access to the corridor beyond to account for all those doors.

The light was better than up in the room Edward was in, but it was still more gloom and shadow than visible objects. Something at the foot of one of the beds was catching the light. Something metallic. More manacles, I guessed.

At least they were treating Edward and Thomas the same in that much. But Thomas had gotten the much nicer room.

I didn't see anything moving in the shadows, and once I had my own breathing under control, I heard no one else in that room with me. Whoever I had seen looking down at me seemed to be quite gone now.

A cold breeze was moving through the room, stirring the curtains and the bedclothes. I crossed from the window to the open French doors that led out onto the balcony.

There was a cast iron table and a pair of chairs in one corner of the balcony, nicely situated for someone to enjoy a cup of coffee, perhaps even breakfast, while watching the sun rise over the river valley. But no one came out here in the winter, to judge by the depth of the unshoveled snow.

Unshoveled, but not unmoved. I wouldn't describe what I was looking at as footprints, exactly. More like someone had been dragged, and he had struggled a lot. I could see the patch of the balcony where he had gone over, now clear of snow.

I heard the sound of someone unlocking the door behind me, but I was too far away to make it back out the window. I could possibly duck behind one of the chairs or under one of the beds, but that would only buy me a little time.

I turned to face the door as the knob started to turn. I was tempted to draw my wand in case it was the murderer returning to the scene of the crime, but that wasn't likely to do me any good if it was and would be downright embarrassing if it was anyone else coming into the room.

The door swung open, filling the room with a dazzling amount of light. I could hear several voices, male voices, but the talking died away as the first ones in stopped moving and everyone behind piled into them.

"What's she doing in here?" someone asked.

"Where's Thomas?" someone else asked.

"Did she let him go?"

"How? I have the only key." I was pretty sure I recognized that voice as belonging to Stuart. I shaded my eyes from the brightest of the light and squinted into the crowd of shadows advancing on me.

"What are you doing here?" This one stepped close enough to block out the light behind him, and I recognized McConnell's face with its generous dusting of freckles.

"I thought I saw someone in here, but it was empty when I came in," I said.

"No one was supposed to go in here. Thomas was being held here," Stuart said, bending to pick up a manacle.

"Don't you know?" I looked at the men milling around the room, checking behind chairs and under beds and inside closets. They didn't seem to know. "Thomas is dead. He fell onto the patio and broke his neck."

"What?" Stuart cried, and before I could stop him, he raced out onto the veranda, trampling through all the marked snow.

Oh well. It's not like it had told me anything I hadn't already known.

"How is he?" Stuart called down.

"Dead!" Sophie yelled back up to him.

He turned away from the railing and came back into the room. "How did this happen?"

"It looked like there'd been a struggle," I said.

"How do you figure that?" he asked.

"The snow you just walked back and forth over," I said. He looked back at the snow and blanched. "It looked like he was dragged to the railing and then tossed over, head first. He might have lived if he hadn't landed on the back of his neck."

Stuart stopped looking at the snow and came to stand intimidatingly close to me, squeezing my arm tightly as he glared into my eyes. "Who did this?"

"I didn't see who," I said, forcing myself to remain calm. But people grabbing me tended to make me angry.

"Stuart, let her go," McConnell said softly. Stuart ignored him.

"You saw something," he said, squeezing me harder.

"I saw someone's head," I said. "Why don't you go downstairs and have one of these other fellows look down at you, just for a moment. Then you can come back and tell me how many identifying features you can be certain you saw."

"You're telling me you've got nothing? You don't know if he was tall or short, thick or thin, old or young? Nothing?"

"I couldn't even be sure he was a he," I said. He let me go with a little flinging gesture that might have knocked back a less sturdy woman.

"I can tell you one thing," I said. "It wasn't Edward."

"How do you figure that?"

"Because Edward is still upstairs, under lock and key," I said.

"She has a point there," McConnell said.

"Someone, go check," Stuart said, and one of the men closer to the door ran out into the corridor. I could just hear the sound of his footsteps on the stairs.

Then I remembered that as much as the door was locked and there were two guards still on duty, I had taken off Edward's manacles. If anyone noticed that detail and chose to focus on it, I might have just made everything a lot more difficult for team Exonerate Edward.

If I hadn't let Stuart make me so mad, I might have figured out a way to get upstairs and lock him back up before anyone thought to check. Although I don't know how I would have pulled that off. But just thinking about it had me touching my bag again, groping the outline of my wand.

And only my wand.

That wasn't right. I glanced around, but none of the other police were looking at me. McConnell had them in a huddle, sending them off singly and in pairs to handle other tasks. I reached my hand inside the bag. I felt the warmth of the wood of my wand, but that was it.

The key was gone.

I distinctly remembered having it when I left Edward's room. I had touched the bag to be sure it was still in there and that I hadn't left it behind. So when had I lost it?

Then I remembered. Someone had bumped into me in the ballroom. That was a classic pickpocket distraction. Was one of the gangsters a pickpocket before he moved up to bigger crime?

I wracked my brain, but I just couldn't picture who had bumped into me. It had been crowded. I hadn't gotten a good look or even a bad one.

"I'm afraid you'll have to come with me," McConnell said. I flinched when he moved to take my arm, and he stepped back. "Sorry."

"Where are you taking me?" I asked.

"To the library to see the chief."

"I'll walk with you," I said. "I'm not going to run away. In fact, there's nothing I want more right now than to talk to your chief."

He gave me a little nod and then we walked out into the hall and down the corridor towards the bright light of the chandelier in the main hall. McConnell turned towards me to say something but was distracted by staring at my arm.

"I'm terribly sorry," he said, and I glanced down to see dark purple bruises blooming where Stuart's fingers had been.

"It's nothing," I said. "I bruise easy." Years of hockey had taught me that.

"It's not acceptable," McConnell said. "I'll see he's reprimanded."

"I'm not worried about that," I said. "I'm worried about Edward. Please tell me no one is going to leave him alone with my friend."

"No, of course not," McConnell said, but he looked suddenly nervous.

"Please send someone up," I said. "Stuart was angry with me. I don't want to think how he'll be with Edward."

"I'll go up myself as soon as you're in the library," McConnell said. "Edward will be safe. You have my word."

"As an officer of the law?" I asked.

"Yes."

"The law as it's enforced here in St. Paul? Justly and equally to all of its citizens? Me or, say, that fellow over there?" I asked.

I was pointing to Otto leaning against the wall just outside the library doors. He had taken off his tie to staunch a nosebleed.

McConnell stopped dead in his tracks to turn to face me there on the staircase. "I know a lot of my fellow officers are corrupt. I know that corruption runs deep. I know there is nothing in the world that can convince you that I'm not one of those. Even so, I give you my word; I will do everything I can to see that justice is done and that injustice is punished."

A lot of sarcastic responses came to mind, but what good would that do? Instead, I just nodded.

"Thank you, officer. I accept your word and am satisfied."

"Good," he said, blinking in surprise. "Now, let's get you inside the library so I can start running up those stairs."

He crossed the hall to the library doors and knocked loudly. I waited at his elbow, but my eyes were on Otto.

Otto looked a mess. I could see no other visible damage, but from the stiff way he was moving, I knew they had done far more than just broken his nose.

Then Otto saw me standing there, and his eyes widened with panic. I put a finger to my lips, then patted my beaded bag.

He settled back against the wall, calmer now. He nodded at my bag, then pointed at the floor at his feet.

So he trusted me to face the library alone, but he was going to wait right there until I came out again.

"Here we go," McConnell said, as someone inside the library swung open just one of the doors. McConnell stepped back to let me enter. "Tell them everything," he whispered to me.

Then he was gone, running up the stairs. And I alone stepped inside the library.

CHAPTER 17

$\mathcal{I}$ only got the briefest of glimpses of the room filled with books and anxious-looking men before I was nearly bowled over by someone tackling me, arms wrapping tightly around my middle. My body reacted without my brain needing to summon a thought, dropping my center of gravity and planting my feet to brace against the blow.

But the arms around me weren't trying to confine me. I was getting hugged. Almost uncomfortably tightly, but still. I looked down and recognized Coco's dark head.

"Coco?" I said.

She hugged me tighter. Then I saw Charlotte standing behind her, looking at me through narrowed eyes. I patted Coco's shoulder, and she finally let me go.

"I'm sorry." She didn't so much whisper as just mouth the words.

"For what?" I asked, but she just shook her head sorrowfully then stepped around me to leave the library. Charlotte turned her head as she walked past me to keep that glare fixed on me until she too stepped out the door, closing it behind her.

I kept looking at the door, not ready to turn around and face the rest of the room yet. What had Charlotte told them? Given Coco's behavior, it must have been bad.

"Miss Clarke, is it?" someone said to me, and I could delay it no longer. I turned to face the room.

Despite my trepidation, my first thought at getting a good look at the library was how thrilled Brianna would be if she ever got inside. The room extended up to the second story of the house, with a balcony running the perimeter of the room at that level. A fire was hissing and sparking inside the massive fireplace, filling the air with the smell of well-aged wood and smoke. An array of sofas were arranged around the hearth, each crammed with men who had been in tuxedos for the party but were in various stages of undress now, most with their coats off, quite a few with loosened ties or cummerbunds removed, and one or two with the sleeves of their dress shirts rolled up.

Mr. McTavet was sitting behind a massive desk in the center of the room, scraping out the bowl of his pipe with shaking hands. The chief was sitting on one corner of the desk, and a man wearing a black suit but not a tuxedo, and a fedora rather than a top hat was standing behind Mr. McTavet's chair.

The man in the suit was the one who had said my name. He was looking at me now with growing impatience.

"Yes, I'm Amanda Clarke," I said. "McConnell asked me to tell you all what I know about what happened to Thomas."

"We have more questions than that," the man in the suit said, or rather snarled.

"Please be civil, Mr. Reilly," Mr. McTavet said to him, his eyes still on his pipe as he filled it with fresh tobacco. "Miss Clarke is a guest in my house, and I will have her treated as such."

"I wasn't rude," Reilly said, but in a more neutral tone.

"Is she a guest?" the chief asked, turning to look back at Mr. McTavet. "Her name doesn't appear on the list you gave me." He picked up a piece of paper off the desk and gave it a quick scan then shrugged.

"She was a last-minute addition at the request of my daughter," Mr.

McTavet said.

"Ivy?"

"No, Coco."

"I see," the chief said and turned back to face me. "How do you know Coco?"

"I live next door," I said, surprised they didn't already know that. What had Coco and Charlotte told them?

"You seem a little old to be a playmate of Coco's," Reilly said.

"I do believe that my friends and I were invited because we are friends of Edward's," I said. "Coco didn't want him to have no one to stand with him when... well, I guess at the time she thought he was the one getting engaged today."

Mr. McTavet sighed, and both the chief and Reilly looked at him, waiting for him to speak. But he merely lit his pipe then sat back in his chair, smoking.

"Yes, well," Reilly said then consulted a notepad in his hand. "You saw Thomas fall, then?"

"Yes, past the parlor window," I said. "He fell head first. I believe he landed on the back of his neck."

"Swan dive," Reilly muttered, scribbling in his notebook.

"Excuse me?" I said.

"Hitting the ground head first would be the only reason he's dead from that fall," he said.

"You're making it sound like he jumped, Mr. Reilly," I said.

"Yes, that is the theory we're working from," he said.

"You've examined the body?" I asked.

"Of course," he said, narrowing his eyes at me. But I wasn't intimidated.

"Examined it for defensive wounds?"

"I'm the one asking the questions here, missy," he said.

"Then start asking the right ones," I said. "Thomas was thrown from that balcony."

"You saw that from the parlor window, did you? The window which is nearly directly beneath the veranda?"

"No, but I was the first one to reach the body. He was already dead,

127

but when I looked up, I saw someone up there looking down at me."

"Who?" Reilly asked.

"I don't know. Go outside and take a look for yourself. With the light coming from the lanterns around the patio, it's impossible to see more than shadows of everything up on the veranda."

"Then you can't be sure you saw anything at all."

"I know I saw someone. They fled when I noticed them there, and by the time I got up to the room they were gone."

"The room was locked," Reilly said.

"I got in through the window," I said.

"I meant, how did the person you claim to be chasing get out of the room without a key?"

"Perhaps they had a key," I said.

"There are only two keys that work on those doors, and my men had possession of both of them for the entire time," Reilly said.

"Someone got in and out of there somehow," I said. "You can't exactly claim it's unfeasible unless you have an explanation for Thomas getting out of his manacles as well. Someone had access to those keys."

The chief turned to look back at Reilly, both eyebrows lifted as if he too was curious what Reilly had to say in response to that.

"Copies of keys can be made," Reilly said. "For all I know, you have one in your bag there right now."

I clutched that beaded bag tightly, not sure what I would do if they asked me to let them search it. I had nowhere else to hide my wand.

But the shape of the bag in my hands was wrong. Or rather, was right again. Because not only I was feeling the length of my wand, I could feel the magical skeleton key as well.

Had I only imagined I had lost it? Or had whoever taken it when they bumped me in the ballroom returned it just as surreptitiously? Or rather more, as I hadn't noticed anyone bumping me since.

Except Coco. Coco had hugged me for a really long time.

Had Coco taken the key? But she didn't even know it existed. Even if she did, why would she take it?

"Have you had much champagne this evening, Miss Clarke?" Reilly asked.

"Some," I said. "But none since Ivy fell. I'm not now nor was I at any point this evening intoxicated."

"Hm," he said and scribbled in his notebook.

"She doesn't seem tipsy now, Reilly," the chief said. "And if she isn't now, I doubt she was minutes ago when Thomas fell."

"Well, it wouldn't take much, would it?" Reilly said to him. "A bit of champagne, the shock from witnessing two deaths in one night, the poor quality of the lighting."

"There was someone on the balcony," I said. "I didn't imagine it."

"You're sticking to that story, then?" he asked. "Despite the six good officers guarding the doors around that room not seeing this supposed person who would have had to get past them to escape?"

"They might not have had to use one of the doors," I said. "This house is filled with secret passages and hidden doors."

"Built for children," Reilly said.

"I can fit through them," I said, then instantly regretted it. The last thing I needed was to put myself on the suspect list. Reilly looked me up and down, eyes lingering on the skirt of my gown that was torn in several places, wet from the snow, and covered in dust from crawling through the passage out of Coco's room. And below that, my dirty, bare feet.

"It looks like you have at that," he said.

"Why are we arguing about this when you should be searching the house?" I asked. "The murderer is still among us, undetected by any of you, and perhaps about to strike again."

"I'm sorry, miss, but I just don't find your story convincing," he said. "We've searched the entire room and the rooms around it, and there is no sign of any person lurking anywhere. No one was in that room but Thomas. That is a fact, and facts are all I have to work with."

"That makes no sense," I said. "Thomas set himself free of his manacles how exactly?"

"Thomas was a man of wide-ranging interests," Reilly said with a shrug.

"Lockpicking as well as boxing?" I asked.

"Perhaps he was a fan of Houdini. Many his age were when they were young."

"Those are your facts?" I scoffed. He narrowed his eyes at me again.

"He was alone. That is a fact until we find proof otherwise."

"Are you saying he freed himself from his bonds then went out on the veranda to take the air and accidentally fell – head first, no less – over the rail?" I asked.

"No," Reilly said, his eyes mere slits now.

"I say," Mr. McTavet interjected. "Look here, Reilly, if you're saying the young man offed himself, I really must object. Think of his family."

"We would need proof before I will tell them any such thing," the chief said.

"It's more likely than an accidental death," Reilly said. "Look, I hate it as much as both of you, but we can't rule it out. He was a boy of strong passions. The love of his life was just killed before his eyes. We know he felt guilt for his powerlessness to save her. He was frozen like a statue until our boys put hands on him, but then he was raving when we locked him in the room."

"We should have spoken with him sooner," the chief said, and Mr. McTavet made a murmuring sound of agreement.

"Are you going to argue that he wasn't despondent?" Reilly asked me.

"I never met him when he was still alive," I said. I too wished I had spoken with him sooner. "But from what I've heard, those strong passions you mention were more of the angry sort."

The chief pinned Reilly with a look again.

"We never did rule him out as a suspect to my satisfaction," Reilly said. "He could have killed Ivy in a fit of passion then offed himself in regret."

"Let's not pursue this line of thought any further," the chief said.

"But it fits the facts better than an accident," Reilly said.

"Someone else was up there with him, I'm telling you," I said. "Since you won't take my word for it, it really is a shame that your man Stuart trampled over the snow on the veranda, or you could've seen the signs of a struggle for yourself."

"Yes, a shame," Reilly said as if he had found another hole in my story.

"Didn't you talk to Coco?" I asked. "Didn't she tell you about the person that was up on the balcony with them, that knocked her to the ground just before Ivy fell?"

"She mentioned that," Reilly said with a look on his face like he'd just been sucking on a lemon.

"For someone who insists you work with facts, it sure looks to me like you only accept as fact the things that fit your pet theory," I said.

"Careful with your tone," Reilly said.

"Reilly, we're not going to call this a suicide unless we're absolutely sure," the chief said. "And accidental death seems unlikely. Someone here has a motive to kill Thomas and Ivy both on their engagement day. The announcement took many by surprise, but for someone, it wasn't a happy one. Let's go over the witness statements again with fresh eyes. Oh, and Miss Clarke? You can go rejoin the rest of the party in the ballroom."

"You should keep everyone together in groups," I said. "In case the killer isn't finished."

The chief raised his eyebrows at me. "We did tell everyone to stay in a group in the ballroom after the first death this evening. It's just you and your friends that didn't get that message."

I felt my cheeks coloring. He was right.

"The witness statements can wait," Reilly said, flipping through his notebook. "Let's take a closer look at that veranda. Stuart might not have trampled on all of the evidence."

"Upstairs, then," the chief said, standing up and stretching out his back. The others got up from the sofas, and Mr. McTavet got up from his chair.

"One more thing?" I said as the chief walked past me. He looked back at me, less patient this time. "We can agree that Edward could not possibly be the one who killed Thomas, correct?"

"He could still have killed Ivy," Reilly said. "We haven't ruled out two killers."

"But the person who killed Thomas was capable of sneaking past guards and locked doors to get to him. Edward might be in danger. As his friend and a profound believer that his innocence will be proven, I'm asking you to let him come downstairs. Shackle him in the ballroom if you like. Just put him in a place where many eyes can watch over him. You can be sure he doesn't kill, and I can be sure he isn't killed himself."

"Fair enough," the chief said. "Jerry, go up there and tell the boys to bring him down."

The young man he was looking at nodded and pushed his way to the front of the crowd to be the first to run up the stairs.

And just like that, I was alone in the library. I opened my bag and looked inside to be sure I hadn't imagined it. But no, the key was definitely there.

The fire was still hissing and popping, but I thought I heard something else, a softer sound. Like a skirt brushing against a wall, maybe? I crept closer to the fireplace, straining my ears in case the sound should come again.

Coco had a listening place somewhere in the walls around this room. Was it near the fireplace? Were she and Charlotte in there now?

Charlotte. If she had told the police what she had seen the three of us doing at the top of the stairs, they clearly hadn't taken her seriously, or they would have asked me about it.

But why would she keep our secret?

CHAPTER 18

I was still moving slowly and silently around the library, looking for signs of little doors and listening for anything moving within the walls when the door to the hall slammed shut.

"Sorry," Sophie said when I jumped and spun around, brandishing my beaded bag as if it were a weapon. "Heavy door."

"Woah," Brianna said as her eyes grew huge. She looked just like Beauty when the Beast shows her his library. She was up on her toes, turning and turning to try to see everything at once. I was afraid she was about to burst into song.

"Where are Coco and Charlotte?" I asked.

"Coco is in the ballroom with her mother," Sophie said, handing me my sodden shoes. "The police are keeping everyone confined to the ballroom now. No one is allowed upstairs or even in the parlor."

"And yet we're all here," I said, slipping my shoes on. Not that they warmed up my feet at all. What I really wanted was a bath.

"Yeah," Sophie said with a humorless laugh. "Ricci was at the door when we asked to come in and get you since we were pretty sure you'd been left behind in here. He pretended to be against the idea, but he wasn't very convincing."

"So what's that mean?" I asked.

"They think we're involved in all of this," Brianna said. "They're hoping to use us as bait to flush out the murderer."

"Why would they think that?" I asked.

"Maybe because we're the only ones here for Edward?" Sophie said.

"Did you see him? They promised to bring him downstairs," I said.

"No, but maybe he's still on his way down," Brianna said.

"Coco and Charlotte were in here just before I was," I said. "Coco told me she was sorry, but I have no idea why. I thought Charlotte had said something, but if she outed us as witches, no one said anything about it."

"Why would they believe her?" Sophie asked.

"They know we're from the school, and the school has a reputation," Brianna said. "They might not say anything publicly, they might try to present themselves as rational and logical and not at all superstitious, but I'm pretty sure they're all thinking it. They're watching us for any sign that she's right."

"Assuming she said anything at all," Sophie said.

"Something else strange happened," I said. "Whoever threw Thomas out the window somehow got past the guards without being seen, through locked doors, and got Thomas out of locked shackles before throwing him off the veranda."

"Maybe they climbed down from the third floor?" Sophie said.

"And picked the lock on the shackles?" Brianna said.

"Normally I would think so too," I said. "But the problem is when I was talking to McConnell up in the master bedroom, I realized that the key was missing from my bag. But look." I opened my bag and took out the golden key. "Just now I noticed it was back again."

"Are you sure you didn't just lose track of it?" Sophie asked.

"Completely," I said. "Someone bumped into me when we were in the ballroom. That's when they took it from my bag without me noticing. But I have no idea how they got it back in there. I've been surrounded by cops since I noticed it was gone."

"They took it from you before Thomas was killed?" Brianna said.

"Exactly," I said. "Then put it back when they were done."

"But how would anyone here even know what it was?" Brianna asked.

"You should be grateful they didn't take your wand," Sophie said.

"I wished you would have been able to tell us as soon as you noticed it was gone," Brianna said. "I could have done a tracing spell to find it."

"I could have found it myself if I had a chance to go to the world of threads. It glows like a sun there. But there was no time."

"I wonder if the thief knew that," Sophie said. "They returned it before we could trace it because they knew we could find them out that way."

"Is there a spell we can do to trace who had it?" I asked. "Maybe the pathway of where it went when it wasn't in my bag."

"Or I could identify the energy of the person who was holding it," Brianna said. "Let me think."

But the moment those words were out of her mouth there was a loud knocking at the door.

"Someone must think the police are still in here," I said.

"I'll shoo them away," Sophie said and went to answer the door. I put the key in Brianna's hands, and she slipped it out of sight into her own bag. We both looked up as Sophie stepped aside to let Otto into the library, followed closely by Edward.

"Edward! Why are you here and not in the ballroom?" I asked. "Please tell me you are not bait too."

"Who is bait?" he asked. Even in the warm light from the fireplace and the soft glow from the gaslights he looked a sickly sort of pale.

"It's just a theory," Sophie said. Edward more fell into than sat on one of the sofas. Otto went over to Mr. McTavet's desk and started touching the inkstand and pipe rack and other items on its surface as if he were shopping in a store. Brianna was tapping her hand on the side of her beaded bag as if counting her thoughts.

"I have to… check something," she said.

"Oh, you thought of something about the… thing?" I finished lamely.

"I need a quiet place," Brianna said. "Perhaps as bait, I'll be allowed the use of the parlor."

"Be careful," Otto said, his words muffled. He had put one of Mr. McTavet's pipes in his mouth.

"Why don't we go with her," Sophie suggested. "I can help, and you can stand guard."

Otto looked like he wanted to refuse, but Sophie tipped her head in Edward's direction ever so slightly. I hadn't told them that I had already done magic in front of Edward, so I could see why she thought we still had to shield him from it. But from the slow smile that spread across Otto's face, he took a different meaning from her gesture.

"It's perfectly quiet in here," I said, but Sophie shook her head at me.

"We'll be back in a jiff," she said.

"Don't follow any leads without me," I said.

"Of course not," Sophie said. "Unless I stumble over that Charlotte girl. If I do, she's definitely going to be telling me everything she's been telling everybody else, whether they believed her or not."

"Fair enough," I said.

The door closed behind them, and I was alone in the enormous but strangely comfy library with Edward.

"Did McConnell get upstairs in time?" I asked, settling onto the edge of the sofa across from Edward.

"In time for what?" he asked.

"I got the sense that that Stuart fellow wanted to hurt you," I said. "You heard about Thomas?"

"Yes," Edward said. "I don't understand what's happening here. Who would want to kill Ivy and Thomas? It defies reason."

"I was afraid they'd still blame you, especially once they found you unshackled."

"I wasn't unshackled," he said and mustered something of a smile. "I heard them rattling at the door and locked myself back up before they came in."

"That was clever of you," I said.

"I didn't want to get you in trouble," he said. "Not that they knew you were even in there."

"I asked them to let you go since whoever killed Ivy probably also killed Thomas, and that one couldn't have been you," I said. "But I don't think they've stopped trying to find a way to pin it on you."

"They're working the case," Edward said. "It's not the all-out scape-goating of me that Otto likes to paint it as."

"No, I suppose not," I said.

"I've been going over and over that moment in my head," Edward said. "Since we talked about it together."

"When Ivy fell?" I asked. "Do you remember another person up there now?"

"No, not that moment," he said. "The one just before."

"I don't understand," I said.

"I'm not saying it very well," he said and sighed. His eyes were fixed on the hands on his lap. He was slowly opening and closing them, an unsettling gesture.

"Edward?"

"I was thinking about what I felt the moment when Mr. McTavet announced that Ivy was betrothed to Thomas. That moment."

"Oh," I said. This wasn't going to be helpful information to the investigation then. "I was under the impression you already knew what was going to be announced."

"Yes. Ivy had told me when I arrived for what I thought was going to be our engagement party," he said. "She told me, but it was like I didn't quite hear. Like the words went through my ears, but my mind just held onto them. Like a letter I intended to open later."

"I don't suppose Ivy gave any hint that she might be in danger?" I asked.

Edward seemed to find the question startling, like I had derailed his train of thought. He had to consider it a moment before answering. "No, she didn't say a thing to me like that. She wasn't nervous or anxious or anything. She was just... radiant. She glowed. She was like a pure thing, so very, very happy."

"Ah," I said. Because I had to say something.

"Then I went down to Mr. McTavet's study. He felt badly about how things were being handled, this last-minute switching about of engagements. He was very apologetic and promised over and over that I still had a bright future at the bank. But it was the same thing again. The words went into my ears, but I couldn't make myself quite hear them."

"It sounds like you were in shock," I said.

"Yes," he said. "I think maybe that's what it was."

"I'm sorry," I said. "I know how much you longed for the match, how hard you worked for it. From what little I saw of her, Ivy seemed very lovely. And I know you wouldn't have held her in such high regard if she wasn't worthy of it."

Wow, I almost sounded like I believed that.

"Everyone loved Ivy," he said. "She was the very heart of every room she ever entered."

I had no answer for that. It was getting harder and harder not to admit that I liked Ivy less every time I heard something new about her.

"Yes, I think shock is the word for the state I was in all afternoon," Edward said. "I wandered the upstairs halls; I don't even know why. I really should have just gone home, but Mr. McTavet was so anxious for me to stay. So I lingered. I felt like a ghost, like I was already haunting Thomas and Ivy and would for the rest of my days.

"But then Mr. McTavet made his announcement. He said those words. He said their names together. And that time I heard it. I really heard it. Thomas and Ivy were going to be husband and wife. And such a feeling came over me out of nowhere. I hadn't expected to feel anything like it."

I reached out and caught his hand, very afraid of what he was going to say next.

"Please don't," I said. "You don't have to tell me."

"I want to," he said, squeezing my hand back.

"No. Don't confess. Don't tell me what feelings overwhelmed you. Nothing you can say is going to make me blame you for what happened. I know you didn't do it."

"What are you talking about?" he asked.

"Anger?" I said. "I'm sure you felt betrayed. I can understand feeling anger. Even a desire for revenge would be quite understandable in those circumstances. But don't tell me. I need to remain impartial, right?"

"But I wasn't feeling any of those things," Edward said. "The feeling that washed over me out of nowhere was relief. All of my hopes and dreams had been thoroughly, cruelly destroyed, and yet in the moment when I accepted that was true, and it was all over, all I felt was relief."

CHAPTER 19

*E*dward was still looking at his hands, although they now just rested half-open in his lap. He had stopped flexing them over and over. He seemed at peace.

But I was glad he wasn't looking at me. My heart had stopped beating for a moment, and I wasn't sure whether my face had gone bright red or ghastly pale, but either way it would be clear my feelings were stomping all over me.

"It was a relief. It was finally over. And I hadn't even realized it was an ordeal," he said. "It's all so strange."

"You don't have to process everything all at once," I said. "It's okay to take your time."

But he didn't seem to hear me. He just kept talking. He kept saying all the words that were making it hard for me to breathe.

"I thought I loved her. I was quite certain of it. I had even had fights with Otto about it. He didn't think I truly loved her. He said she was just a symbol of the life I wanted. I don't think that's true, even now. She's not a symbol to me."

"Otto was just trying to be a good friend," I said. "If you and Ivy had gotten engaged, he would have been the first to congratulate you both."

"Oh, I know. He said his piece, and then he was going to hold his peace. That's how he phrased it. It's just so strange. I was absolutely convinced I spoke from the heart when I argued with him about it. And yet, the moment Mr. McTavet said Thomas and Ivy, their names together, I realized I had never loved her. And I felt relieved that I would no longer think I did. Does that make any sense?"

Then he looked up at me, catching me unawares. I sat back, straight and tall, and made the expression on my face shift to something neutral. I might be thrilled to hear the words that he had never loved Ivy, but I couldn't let that show. Not to him.

"Wait a minute," I said, shifting my attention to all the other words he had been saying. "Are you saying you were under a spell?"

He blinked, confused, then nodded. "Yes, I guess that's one way to describe it. It felt like I had been under a spell and then it was broken. Just like that."

"It felt like, or it *was* like?" I asked.

"What are you asking me, Amanda?" he asked. "I know you're not teasing me. Not now."

"No, I'm not teasing," I said. "I just thought maybe you were telling me that Ivy put a spell on you."

"Like something out of a song," he said. "But no, not Ivy. Ivy just… changed her mind."

"Maybe you're just having a manic response," I said.

"What does that mean?" he asked.

"Maybe your feelings will switch on a dime again, and you'll feel all the sadness all at once."

"I don't think so," he said. "No, that's not what I'm feeling. I truly am relieved. I wanted nothing more than to wish Thomas and Ivy every happiness in the world. If anything, I'm sad I didn't get a chance to do that."

"It is a shame," I agreed.

"I'm not sad about losing Ivy," he said, looking at me intently. "She wasn't the one for me."

I shot up from the sofa and moved closer to the fireplace, to turn my back on those eyes and whatever he was about to say next. But even with my back turned, he could keep talking. I needed to steer the conversation in a different way.

"You are taking it all better than Mary Taylor," I said. "She's quite distraught. Do you know Mary?"

"A little," he said. "She was always close to Ivy."

"Ivy didn't tell her she was changing who she was getting engaged to," I said. "Mary didn't find out until the announcement, in front of everyone. She was crushed."

"She had feelings for Thomas? I had no idea," Edward said.

"I'm not sure Thomas did either, unfortunately," I said.

"It's better not to wait with such things," he said, and his voice was much closer. He was standing just behind me, and I could feel him willing me to turn around.

"*Was* there anyone else?" I asked, a sudden thought striking me.

"What?" he asked.

"Was there anyone else caught up in this love tangle? You with Ivy, Ivy with you and Thomas, Thomas with Ivy and Mary. Was there another person caught up in this somewhere? Perhaps loving from afar? Someone with a temper and a desire for revenge, perhaps?"

Now I did turn to face him, but only to be sure he was listening to me.

He was. His face was serious as he thought it over.

"You've been to all the parties, all the afternoon gatherings. Ivy had a lot of other suitors, right?" I said.

"I'm thinking who else I saw here," he said. "There were a few more men who were pursuing her with great seriousness. On their part. Ivy liked the attention, but she didn't encourage it when she wasn't prepared to return it."

"Did you know she was encouraging Thomas?" I asked.

"No," he admitted.

"Then there might have been others."

"No, I don't think so. Thomas is… was different. They had a closeness from being childhood friends. He never called on her as a suitor that I know of."

"Still, if you can think of any names, that could be useful," I said.

"There are so many places to hide in this house, so many ways to get in besides the front door. The person who did this might not have even had an invitation. But they could still be here now. Edward, you could be a target."

"I don't think so," he said. "I don't feel like I'm in danger."

I clenched my hands in fists to keep from tearing at my hair. What I really wanted in that moment was to hear a little less about Edward's feelings. It was all too much.

"Please, stick close to Otto," I said. "And speaking of, we should go find him now. It's not safe for the two of us to be on our own."

"Wait," he said, catching my wrist before I could head to the door.

"Edward, this isn't the time," I said.

"It has to be the time," he said. "I have to tell you-"

"Please don't," I said.

"Amanda," he said, taking a step closer.

"Edward," I said, putting my hand on his and removing it from my wrist. He let it drop to his side, but the hurt in his eyes was going to kill me. "You said all you wanted in the world was to wish Thomas and Ivy joy on their engagement. And I know that feeling. Because I came here with that same desire. To wish you and Ivy joy. And I'm sad for you that it all ended so badly."

"You won't even let me say the words?" he asked.

"Please don't," I said. "They won't change anything. They'll just make it harder for both of us."

"Amanda-" he started to say.

I had never been so pleased to see a dozen police officers pour into a room before. They banged into the library, knocking both doors wide open, their voices loud and boisterous as they headed for the places, they had only just left moments before on the sofa and around the desk.

Edward stepped back from me and thrust his hands into his pockets. Only the chief seemed to notice how close we had been standing together by the fireplace, but he only raised an eyebrow. He didn't say a thing.

"Oh good, Scott, you're here," Reilly said as he came through the doors. "We had some more questions for you."

"I'm happy to help," he said then glanced at me. "Miss Clarke had an interesting theory."

"You can fill us in on that yourself, I'm sure. Miss Clarke has to rejoin the others in the ballroom now," Reilly said, putting a hand on the small of my back to steer me towards the door.

"Don't hurt him," I hissed at Reilly.

"Madam, I'm an officer of the law," he said.

"I know," I said and shot him a look.

"That's enough of that," he said, then gave me a little push to keep me moving past the door. "Go on into the ballroom now. There's cake, and it's nearly midnight. Keep walking. I'm not closing these doors until I see you safely through those doors."

I felt the rush of anger throughout my body, the blood in my ears singing, my heart thumping like a war drum. Then I felt my hair prickling up like from static and forced myself to calm down. This wasn't the time or place to unleash all of my power.

At least, not yet.

CHAPTER 20

The ballroom was as far from a party atmosphere as it was possible to get. Mrs. McTavet, having been brought down from her private rooms by the police, was loudly grieving in the corner near the band. They had stopped playing and were sitting together on the far side of the little stage. Coco was sitting near her mother, trying and failing to be any comfort at all.

An older woman was encouraging Mrs. McTavet to drink more from a cup that I dearly hoped held more than mere tea. Her guests were already on edge from their long entrapment. Her tears were making the situation near intolerable. Many of the women were starting to cry as well. The men looked like they were fixing to make another attempt at getting past the guards at the door. It was getting easier to tell who of the remaining partygoers were gangsters and who were more mundane businessmen.

I didn't linger. No one was near Coco, not Brianna or Sophie or even Charlotte, and I wished I could do something for her, but I had other duties that had to come first.

As much as the chief had said everyone was to be confined to the ballroom, the two guarding the door to the back corridor didn't even look up as I passed between them.

But when I reached the parlor, I found it empty.

I hesitated in the doorway. Had I somehow missed seeing Brianna and Sophie in the ballroom? No. With Sophie in that eye-catching red dress, there was no way I wouldn't see her if she was there. Or Otto in his bottle-green suit, for that matter.

The spell must have worked. They must be in pursuit of the murderer even as I stood there uselessly in the doorway.

I went into the parlor and sat down in one of the wing-backed chairs. It would only take a moment. I would pop into the world of threads and look around. Brianna and Sophie, I would know at once, and the key itself glowed like a beacon. I only needed a moment.

But the moment my eyes closed, before I had even steadied my breath, I heard the sound of the parlor door clicking shut. As if someone was trying to do it stealthily.

To trap me in there.

I had forgotten that I was bait.

I stood up from the chair, one hand holding my bag and the other inside of it, groping for my wand, but both hidden from view of the door by the back of the chair.

"Oh," I said when I saw who was there. It was Charlotte. "I hope we didn't frighten you before, up on the stairs. Or perhaps you've already run into Sophie and Brianna, and they explained?"

She didn't answer, just stood there looking at me. I could read no emotion on her face. The single lamp still burning in the room cast more shadow than light, but I could still see her face well enough that I should have gotten some clue as to what she was thinking or intending.

"Are you looking for Mary?" I asked. Which was a silly thing to ask. What if she said yes? I had no idea where Mary was. Searching with the others?

"I know Mary isn't here," Charlotte said. Her voice was as flat as her face was blank. She was starting to creep me out.

I went ahead and took out my wand. I let her see it. She glanced at it, but only for a split second.

"What do you want, Charlotte?" I asked. She took a step closer to me, shoving a mass of loose hair out of her eyes.

"You got so close to the answer, but then you danced away," Charlotte said.

"What are you talking about?" I asked.

"Before, when you were in the library talking to Edward," she said and took another step closer.

I held the wand up higher. "You were listening from that cubby."

"Of course I was .You heard me in there," Charlotte said, unbothered. As she moved her face fell into shadow, but the light shone on her legs. The hem of her skirt was torn, and her shoes looked like mine: quite ruined by the snow.

"When were you outside, Charlotte?" I asked.

"It doesn't matter," she said. She started to take another step but froze when I thrust the wand out towards her.

"Not another step," I said. "Speak your piece, but do it from there."

"I wonder what you can really do with that thing?" she said.

"Finish what you were saying," I said. "You were listening to Edward and me talking. You said I was close to something."

"Yes," she said. "You wanted him to help you figure out who the extra person was that was tangled up in all of the mess. The one that threw all of the love matches out of alignment."

"That's not what I said. We were trying to figure out who the murderer was."

"Well, that's not a mystery any longer, is it?" Charlotte asked.

I reckoned it wasn't. Charlotte was up on the balcony when Ivy fell. Coco couldn't conceive of her friend doing such a thing, but looking at her now I had no problem believing that Charlotte had knocked Coco to the ground and then thrown Ivy over the balcony.

It was easier to see the size of her now that her ill-fitting dress was torn. She had looked round and soft before, but now I could see she was short but stocky. The largeness of her limbs was all muscle. Ivy would have been easy.

She must have lured Thomas into a false sense of security somehow. But I could imagine if he were near the rail already and she caught him off guard, she could upend his feet and send him over head-first. I could imagine it all too clearly.

But there was no reason to say any of that out loud.

"Then what are you teasing me about?"

"The extra person," Charlotte said, growing impatient now. "The one who destroyed everything. The one that drove Edward away from Ivy, the one that made Ivy take Thomas instead when he was meant to be with Mary."

"I thought you hated Thomas," I said.

"It doesn't matter how I felt! He belonged to Mary!"

"All right," I said as soothingly as I could.

I really hoped that spell had worked. Because if it had, then the others would be on their way back to this room now.

"We can't make other people love whom we want them to love," I said. "Thomas might never have chosen Mary even if he was free to do so."

"He would have," Charlotte said.

"And Edward didn't drive Ivy away. He loved her. You heard that yourself if you were listening."

"He says he never did. And I could tell he never did. And so could Ivy. Ivy knew he didn't love her, not really. That's why she finally turned to Thomas."

"Edward is not to blame for all of this," I said.

"We agree on that," she said.

"You stole my key," I said. She just grinned at me. "How did you know I had it, or what it did?"

She grinned wider. "I'm not allowed to tell you that," she said.

"Not allowed by who?" I asked. She said nothing. But she tipped her head to one side and something golden around her neck caught the light. A locket hung at her throat, dangling from a choker. Had she had that before? No, I was sure she hadn't.

I gripped my wand more tightly. Her eyes darted over to it, noticing my movement.

"You know who's to blame?" she asked.

"You are," I said. "Although how murdering your sister's best friend and secret love is supposed to make her life in any way better is beyond me."

"No!" Charlotte shouted at me. "You are! You're to blame. If you hadn't turned Edward's head, we'd all be in the other room celebrating their happy engagement and waiting to count down to the new year. If only you didn't exist!"

Before I could reply, she charged me, throwing the chair aside to tackle me.

As I fell to the floor, my wand flew from my hand.

And wherever it landed, I had no clue.

CHAPTER 21

As surprised as I was to find that Charlotte could hit like a linebacker, she was equally surprised to see how quickly I got back to my feet. I'd played hockey all through high school, and while we played clean matches without resorting to all-out brawls, I had still learned how to take a hit.

But I was distracted. As much as my wand didn't feel like my own anymore, I still didn't like not to know where it was. I tried to keep my eyes on Charlotte, hands up to grapple with her if she tried to charge me again, I couldn't resist the urge to glance down in the direction I thought it had fallen.

It only took a fraction of a second to see that it wasn't under the tea table, but that was all it took for Charlotte to knock me down again. I curled into a ball, protecting my stomach as I fought to catch my breath.

Charlotte stood over me with menacing fists, waiting for me to get up again. She was clearly psychopathic, but not the sort of psychopath who would kick you in the kidneys when you're down. Which was good for me since I couldn't get my diaphragm to calm down and stop spasming.

Then I saw my wand under the desk that sat between the two

windows. I scrambled for it, but Charlotte caught me by the hair and drew me up short. Then she pulled me to my feet. She was quite a bit shorter than me, so rather than standing, I was mostly bent over, trying to get her fingers out of my hair.

She let me go with a push that sent me stumbling forward to the window. Before I had quite recovered, she was tackling me again, this time low at the back of my thighs. She got underneath me and heaved me out the still-open window.

I was lucky my neck hadn't snapped like Thomas'. But my head had plowed through the snow mounded up against the house and struck something hard and rock-like underneath. I rolled away from the window and tried to get up on my hands and knees to crawl, but my vision was nothing but darkness and exploding stars. I only had the vaguest sense of where I was going.

Then my hand landed on Thomas' icy cold ankle. No one had moved his body, although I felt a blanket that might have been draped over him at some point. The wind had blown it half off him.

The band was playing again, and I could hear voices chanting in unison. The countdown. Nearly midnight.

I heard Charlotte's feet hit the snow as she jumped out the window after me. What had taken her so long? I shook my head to clear my vision then looked back at her.

She had my wand in her hand. I felt a wave of revulsion. As if it hadn't been sullied enough already.

She tromped through the snow until she was standing over me, still on my hands and knees in the snow next to Thomas' body. She raised the wand with a look of triumph on her face. I almost wanted to laugh. Clearly, she thought that it would be just like the key, that having it meant she could use it. She looked genuinely confused when nothing happened.

"It needs words too, I suppose?" she said to me.

"It needs more than that," I said.

"Pity," she said and tossed it aside. It plunged into the snow some-where far from the patio lights.

I got to my feet but still needed my hands to keep moving, stumbling past a row of ornamental trees wrapped in canvas for the winter to the deeper parts of the garden.

"I don't need spells to kill you," Charlotte said, plunging her hand into the snow and coming up with a rock from the landscaping. I ducked, putting my arms over my head and trying to turn away. It struck my shoulder and bounced high into the air. I could feel blood welling out of a gash just out of my line of sight, running down the back of my gown.

I kept moving. I don't know that I had a destination in mind. Perhaps there was a way to get over the wall and escape to the charm school.

But to my delight, I saw that past a second row of ornamental trees was a long, narrow skating rink. Someone kept it neatly brushed of snow, and the ice sparkled even in the inadequate light from the house through the trees.

I could hear Charlotte running up behind me, looking to tackle me again. But I wasn't just going to stand there and take another hit. I pushed off from the snowbank and slid out onto the ice, turning as I slid to see Charlotte draw up short.

My shoes only had little kitten heels, but it was more heel than I was used to skating in. And it had been more than a year since I had been out on the ice at all. But my muscle memory was strong. I kept myself sliding, moving backward so I could keep my eyes on Charlotte.

She tried to step out onto the ice after me, but her first step sent her feet up into the air and the rest of her down hard on her butt on the ice. She yelped, more angry than hurt.

I don't think I laughed out loud. I might have smirked. But whatever I did, Charlotte was purple with rage as she got back to her feet. I couldn't quite make out what she was grumbling, but I'm sure if she were a comic strip character it would be written all in grawlix.

"Magic isn't my only talent," I said.

"I have talents as well," she said, still seething. She was feeling all over her skirt, although I couldn't tell if she was searching her pockets or checking for bruises.

"Yes, you're quite the little pickpocket," I said.

"Yes, I am," she said and drew up straight before aiming a gun at me.

"Where did you get that?" I asked.

"Somebody's pocket," she smirked.

"Don't," I said, holding up my hands. As if they could stop a bullet.

The gun went off with a surprisingly soft bang. Then my ear was on fire. The bullet had only grazed me, across my cheek and over the top of my ear, but it was bleeding like crazy, and the pain was searing.

I had to straighten up. I had to get running before she fired again. But I couldn't make myself do it. I couldn't even take my hand off my bleeding ear. She was going to fire again, and there I was without even my traitorous wand to protect me.

The world was going dark again, but this time there were no exploding stars. It was like something was generating clouds of darkness, inky blackness that swallowed the world around me.

Wait, I was the one generating the darkness.

"You're in a sticky spot here," a voice said. I looked up, still clutching my ear. The voice wasn't coming from where Charlotte was standing, still aiming at me, although she appeared to be frozen in time. And it wasn't coming from the house behind her.

I looked to my left, towards the charm school. I could see the ethereal glow of the time bridge that dominated its back yard. The soft pulsation of its threads was stronger than ever now. Then something was emerging from it, a being of light walking towards me without leaving a mark on the mounds of snow.

"Juno," I said.

"I can help you," she said. "I can always help you and always will. You have only to ask."

"No," I said. "I'm good."

"Are you?" Juno said, tipping her head as if to get a better look at my ear.

"I don't need your help," I said.

"No, that's true," she said. "I saw what you did just a few months ago. The power you drew on then, it was impressive. Won't you reach for it now?"

"No," I said. "I don't need that either."

"Really?" Juno said. "You're going to do what exactly?"

I had no idea, and I was sure that the smile I gave Juno was more than a little manic. "Just watch me," I said.

"Always, my protégé," she said. She raised her arms and tendrils of threads from the fabric of the bridge caught her up and pulled her back into the bridge itself.

But I knew she was still watching me. She was always watching me.

The moment I blinked and time started moving forward again the gun went off. I flinched, but this time the whistle of the bullet passed by me.

Charlotte looked at the gun as if it were the gun's fault. She gave it a shake then straightened her arm to take aim again.

But by that time I was already halfway back across the ice. She tried to adjust her aim, but I was jinking back and forth too aggressively for her to get a bead on me. And she waited until too late to think about backing up.

I launched off of the ice with a scream and caught Charlotte around her waist, tackling her back into the snow. The gun went off again, but this shot was truly wild. The air left her in a whoosh when she hit the ground, and the gun went flying out of her hand.

I sat down on her chest, pinning her arms down with my knees. She was struggling like a wild thing, and it took all of my attention just to stay on top of her.

There was nothing to do but wait for her to tire herself out. She wasn't going to be able to dislodge me.

"I say, is someone out there?" a man called.

It took three gunshots in the backyard to draw everyone's attention? What was the point of bait if you weren't keeping an eye on it?

I could hear multiple footsteps coming out of the house, running over the swept patio then into the deeper snow and finally rustling through the trees.

But the first to burst out into the open space around the skating rink was Stuart. He took one look at me pinning Charlotte down and not letting her move. Then he looked at the gun laying in the snow within reach of either of us.

And from the way he narrowed his eyes at me, I knew he had come to the exact wrong conclusion.

CHAPTER 22

"She's got a gun!" Stuart cried as other officers started flowing in through the trees. I leaned into my knees to keep Charlotte pinned down, but I raised both my hands as a dozen men surrounded me with their own guns aimed at me.

"She took it from one of you," I said. "She shot me."

Stuart looked skeptical, but he was standing on the right side of me. McConnell on my left grimaced.

"Get off her!" Stuart commanded.

"Don't let her get away," I said. "She's the killer."

"She's just a kid," one of the other officers said.

"Get up!" Stuart said again.

"If she runs, she'll disappear," I said. "She knows this house better than any of you."

"Pull her off the girl," Stuart said. Two of the officers holstered their weapons then took hold of my arms, pulling me back off of Charlotte.

Who immediately popped up and bolted for the house.

"Catch her!" I screamed, but no one made a move to stop her. They were all still aiming their guns at me. "McConnell! Go after her! Don't let her get away!"

"Isn't that Mary's kid sister?" one of the other officers behind me asked. The other turned to answer him, and while their attention was momentarily off me, I slipped out of their hands and ran after Charlotte.

Charlotte let out a very convincing scream of terror that ended in panicked sobs. She ran faster towards the door off the patio, but the adrenaline surging through my body gave me a burst of speed. By the time her hand was on the doorknob, my hand had caught the back of her dress.

She shrieked in panic as if I were about to kill her.

Then hands were on me again, pulling me back until the back of Charlotte's dress slipped from my grasp. But my fingers still had a hold of something that snapped.

I was flung down onto the cold patio flagstones, and once more I had the breath knocked out of me.

Then I was buried under half a dozen bodies, all grabbing my arms and legs and holding me still. Too many of them were on top of my chest, and I was already laboring to breathe. I was going to be smothered.

My consciousness was slipping away when I blinked and found myself in the world of threads. All of the officers piled on top of me, their own threads glowing invitingly. I could move them aside with just a few tugs and pulls.

But I didn't. They didn't understand what was happening and had jumped to the wrong conclusion, but only because Stuart had led them there. And looking at his form now I saw that he wasn't being actually malicious. He just had his baseline suspicions of me set way high, so high that everything seemed to reinforce them in his eyes.

But something under that pile of police officers was glowing in the way only magical objects glowed. Not the key; Brianna had that. And not my wand, lost in the snow.

The necklace. I had torn it from Charlotte's neck when I had grabbed at her dress, and I had it still, clutched tightly in my hand even as I fought to breathe. Definitely magic. Who had given it to her? What had it been meant to do?

That last question I could make a guess at. Our spells hadn't found Charlotte or any sign of her angry, dark heart. Not after she had seen us on the stairs. At some point after that, she must have met another witch. A gift-bearing witch.

I looked to Charlotte. She had moved to the inside of the doorway but was still there, watching me struggle under all those bodies. And I could see her so clearly now.

Her threads were like snakes, a writhing dark mass of twisted, tangled aims. Maybe part of her did believe she did what she did for the sake of her sister. But I could see that deep down that wasn't really true.

She had wanted to kill. It was a desire she had nursed inside herself for a very long time. She had only been waiting for an opportunity. And she had seen it on the balcony when Ivy made such a tantalizing target. Only a little push was needed. With the McTavets involved with each other, Edward and Thomas scuffing, and Coco so blinded by the lights she had lost track of where Charlotte was even standing, it was all too easy.

Then she had gone after Thomas. And then after me.

Next would be Coco. I could see it there, the blackness she was pouring into the threads that connected her with the girl who had been meant to be her friend.

I felt at the threads that radiated out from her form. They were loathsome to touch, but I swallowed down my revulsion. I had to do something, but what?

If I reached inside her and severed those threads, would her desire to kill Coco end?

Maybe, but the desire to kill someone would remain. Those dark threads ran all through her form, strangling the few light ones she still had left. I didn't know how I could take the darkness and not kill the light.

I did know how to stop her heart. And maybe she deserved that. But maybe there was a way to save the light inside her that didn't rely on magic. Maybe she could get some help. I doubted she'd ever be an upstanding, contributing member of society, but some small measure of redemption could still be found for her.

I was still holding those dark threads, uncertain what to do when I suddenly had the acute feeling that I was being watched. There, in the world of webs, eyes were on me.

I expanded my awareness, first back towards the time bridge. When Juno failed to appear, I went wider, encompassing the house, the block, the neighborhood.

I found no one, and yet I still felt watched. Someone, or rather several someones, wanted to see what I would do.

I looked down at Charlotte's heart threads there in my hand. It would be so easy.

But Coco had asked me for justice. And a summary execution without a trial was not justice.

I released the thread and moved away.

The watchers drew closer around me. I couldn't see them. They weren't part of the web of threads, and yet I felt them there. What strange new magic was this?

Then, one by one, they winked out. One of them, neither the first or the last to disappear, first reached down and somehow plucked the glow of the necklace from out of my hand.

When the last was gone, I realized that as much as I had tried to keep count, I had lost my place somewhere. I had no idea how many they were, not even an approximation. The harder I tried to focus on it, the more random the number my brain threw back at me.

I couldn't narrow it down more than to say it was more than one, less than infinity. Clearly more magic at work.

I settled back into my body and opened my eyes to find I was still under a pile of bodies, although my body hadn't been moving the entire time my awareness had been in the world of webs.

"Get off her!" McConnell was yelling. "You're going to crush her. Can't you see that she's innocent?"

"Let her up but cuff her," Stuart said. The weight of their bodies moved off of mine, and someone helped me to sit up. I would have preferred lying down a bit longer. My whole body felt bruised, and the blood from the bullet graze across my cheek had gotten all over my face while under the hog pile.

I opened my hand, but the necklace wasn't there.

"Don't let Charlotte go," I said. My voice came out hoarse, little more than a croak, but McConnell heard me. He looked towards the house in alarm, and I waited for him to say that she was gone.

"We've got her, Amanda," Otto said. I raised my head to see him and Edward coming out of the house, each holding one of Charlotte's arms. She struggled against them, but they held her fast.

"This is nonsense," Stuart said. "She's just a kid."

"You don't think she's strong enough to throw Ivy over a railing? Come hold this arm, then," Otto said as Charlotte pulled him nearly off his feet.

"But why?" Stuart asked.

"She's crazy," I said. "Have her evaluated. I'm sure you'll find she's not sane enough to stand trial."

"Don't listen to her!" Charlotte shrieked, nearly pulling both men off their feet as she struggled to free herself. "Don't you know what she is?"

"Yes," Coco said. She was standing in the snow between Sophie and Brianna, the footprints behind them leading back to the parlor window. Coco looked ineffably sad. "You told them before, but they didn't believe you."

"She's a witch!" Charlotte yelled, trying to point an accusing finger at me. Otto changed his grip on her arm, twisting it up behind her back.

Stuart looked at me as if trying to see if this were true.

"She did say so before," McConnell told him. "She told the chief. Apparently, she caught these three doing spells at the top of the steps."

"Before the murder?" Stuart asked.

"No, after," he said.

I held my breath, but my fingers were tingling as if I could feel the threads without even moving to that other level of consciousness. If things got bad, I might need to do something drastic to get us all out of there.

163

But Stuart only handed me his handkerchief and made a little gesture towards my face.

"They *are* witches!" Charlotte screamed. "I can prove it! She has a wand! I threw it over there in the snow. Go find it! You'll see I'm telling the truth."

Stuart gave a nod to two of the men who scuffled off through the snow to search. Of course, there were lots of ways to explain away a polished bit of wood, including denying it was even mine, but the idea of yet another stranger touching it was threatening to bring the nausea back.

Then Brianna caught my eye and patted the beaded bag she was holding clutched tight to her belly. I could see the shape of her wand in there. But of course, it would have the same shape even if there were two wands in there. She gave me a nod and held up two fingers as if she heard my thoughts.

"What's going on here?" the chief demanded as he and Reilly pushed past the struggling Charlotte to step out onto the patio.

"It was Charlotte," Coco said, pointing at her friend. "She's the one who pushed my sister off the balcony."

"That isn't what you told us before," Reilly said sternly.

Coco drew herself up taller and stepped up to him. "I was in shock. I remembered someone pushing me, but I couldn't remember who. But I remember now. It's all clear. I swear it."

"That might not be enough to convict her," Reilly said to the chief.

"She had a gun," I said. "She took it from one of you. She tried to shoot me."

The chief blanched at the sight of me, but Reilly just asked, "why?"

"She blamed me for Ivy choosing Thomas over Edward," I said.

"But why would she care about that?" he asked.

"Because her sister loved Thomas," I said. "But she didn't really need a reason. She just wanted to kill. Have a psychologist examine her. I'm sure this will never even go to trial."

The chief had a thoughtful look on his face, and although he said nothing, I was pretty sure I knew what he was thinking.

Charlotte telling everyone we were witches had been a really bad idea on her part. It was pretty ironic; the one thing that made her look instantly crazy in everyone's eyes was actually the truth. I would've laughed if my whole body hadn't been hurting so much.

"Let's bring this party back inside," Reilly said. "Bring her to the library for questioning. Fitzpatrick, call into the station for a meat wagon. No reason to keep the bodies around now. Oh, and Coco, your mother has been looking for you. Can you two bring her inside?"

Brianna and Sophie glanced at me, but at my nod, they agreed, and the three of them went back into the house.

"Here," Stuart said, dropping to one knee to unlock the handcuffs around my wrists.

"Thank you," I said. He gave me a curt nod then followed the others back inside the house.

"Let's get you inside as well," Edward said, slipping his hands under my arms to lift me up onto my feet. He reached up to touch my face, but I flinched away. "Sorry. Are you still bleeding?"

"I have no idea," I said.

"Edward, why don't you get some hot water and a cloth from the kitchen? I'll get Miss Amanda settled by the fire in the parlor so she can warm up," Otto said.

"Yes, of course," Edward said. But he didn't let me go until Otto had a hold of my other arm. I would've complained, only I was pretty sure I wasn't going to be standing for long without the support.

Otto led me into the parlor and put me in a chair by the fire, tucking a blanket around my lap then going to shut the window.

"I should just get home," I said. "Clean, dry clothes. Not party clothes. Surely the police are letting us leave now."

"Let him fuss over you a bit," Otto said, sitting down in the chair opposite mine.

"I really don't think that's a good idea," I said. "After everything that's happened, it would be cruel to let him entertain false hopes."

"Do you know what you look like right now?" he asked.

"No," I said. "What difference does that make?"

"You look like you were hit by a truck. Twice," he said.

"I think it might have been three times," I said.

"Three, then," he said. "Only proves my point more."

"And what is your point?"

He glanced toward the door then scooched his chair as close to mine as it could get. "You were hurt badly. I'm guessing she had a gun on you. We heard the shots, and I know it wasn't you firing any of them. That's not your style."

"Yes, we both know my style," I said, but he cut me off.

"That's what I'm saying. Your life was in danger, but you handled it without doing... that thing you did before," he said. "Which I'll always be grateful for, and don't you ever think any different. But if that thing that you did is the reason why you insist on this wall between you and Edward... well."

"It's not the only reason," I said.

Otto opened his mouth to argue, but he didn't get a chance to say a word. Edward bustled in with a basin of steaming water and a stack of cloths on a tray, Sophie and Brianna both fast on his heels.

Between the four of them, I was quite thoroughly fussed over. But between the aches all over my body and the turmoil of my mind, I couldn't really enjoy it.

CHAPTER 23

I remember when I was a kid, year after year struggling to stay awake until midnight. I was in double digits before I could stay awake long enough to see the ball drop in Times Square. A bit older still before I was awake for midnight in my own time zone. What can I say? I'm an early to bed, early to rise type of girl.

This was the most exhausting New Year's ever.

It was nearly two in the morning before the police let everyone leave the house. I understood it. While it was clear that Charlotte wasn't right in the head, it was perhaps less so that she had killed two people that night. The police had wanted to be sure.

But even after Sophie, Brianna and I had dragged ourselves home, first to the school and then through time to the school in the present, 2019 now, the night was far from over for us.

We went straight up to the library, and I told them both everything that had happened while I was in the yard. How someone had told Charlotte about the key and given her the necklace to hide her from us. How Juno had offered me power again, and I had refused it. How I had felt it there for the taking and fought harder to refuse it again.

How I had felt watched.

Sophie grilled me over and over again to see if I could match the number of watchers to the number of spies Otto had seen following him around, but I just couldn't do it. The harder I tried, the more confused it all became.

"This is not good," Brianna said over and over. "Magic that alters perceptions. Not good."

"Evanora was altering the perceptions of the men around her," I reminded her.

"But this is worse," Brianna said. "They were scrambling *your* perceptions."

"And that's bad because I'm a witch? I don't know. I don't feel like I'm any more perceptive than the next person."

"No, Amanda," Sophie said. "Listen to Brianna."

"They weren't just messing with what you were seeing or hearing. You weren't even in your body at the time you were aware of them, right?"

"Yeah," I said, starting to get it.

"They scrambled perceptions few witches have, and they did it while you were there, in the realm that is your particular domain. The web space thingy," Brianna said.

"That's not good," Sophie said.

I had to agree. It felt very not good at all.

"But you encountered Juno first," Brianna said, and she looked if anything even more worried than before.

"But that was nothing," I said. "She offered to help me, but she didn't press. She went right back into the time bridge, and that was it."

"That's suspicious," Sophie said. "Why would she do that? Why bother to show up at all? She didn't offer to help you the last time you were in danger, and you might have said yes that time."

I bit my lip. I definitely would've said yes that time.

"She's connected with these watching witches somehow," Brianna said.

"But she was gone before they arrived," I said. "They never interacted at all."

"And that's just what's suspicious," Sophie said.

I looked around the library, at the wardrobe that still stood next to the table for the newspapers, at the table strewn with Brianna's books and notes, and the smaller desk I used for my own stabs at research.

"We're not making enough progress, are we?" I said. "And my stupid wand is still being stupid."

"We'll fix it," Brianna said. "We'll figure this out."

"But in the meantime," Sophie said, catching my hand to give it a squeeze. "We should stay here. In 2018. Or I guess 2019 now."

"It's too risky for us in 1929 now," Brianna said.

"I agree," I said. "Why are you both looking at me like you're expecting an argument?"

"Obviously because of Edward," Sophie said.

"Believe me, Edward is just another reason not to go back to 1929," I said. "I need to leave him alone so he can move on."

"Poor Edward," Brianna said.

"It's how it has to be," I said.

We sat in silence for a moment. Exhaustion was making my limbs so heavy I just wanted to drift away to sleep there in the chair. I didn't have the strength to make it to my bed.

But there was one more thing to say. "I do have to go back one more time," I said.

"What?" Sophie asked, blinking back awake.

"No," Brianna said.

"Yes," I said. "I have to talk to Coco. We can't just disappear on her. We can't ghost her. I have to say good-bye."

"Perhaps we can send her a letter-" Brianna began.

"No, Amanda is right," Sophie said. "But not right now."

"No, in the morning," I said.

"Too soon," Brianna said. "I need time to craft some spells. I can make a sort of cloaking spell that will keep the witches from noticing you."

"Of course, you can," I said with a weary smile.

It was nearly a week later when Brianna finally felt satisfied with what she had created. It was a literal cloak with spells worked into the fabric and stitching.

"It won't hold up to direct inspection," Brianna said. "If you think a witch sees you, run."

"I will," I promised.

"Also, I want you to cross time using Cynthia's amulet," she said. "Miss Zenobia put powerful protections on that."

"I will," I said.

"And Sophie and I are going to stand one on each end of the bridge and make sure that Juno doesn't interfere," she said.

"My goodness," I said. "Is this all necessary?"

Brianna gave me a very dark look. "We know how powerful they are with perception magic," she said. "Imagine what they can do if they decide to attack you."

I didn't know what to say to that. I just swallowed hard, my throat gone suddenly dry.

Brianna stayed in 2019. She had doubled the number of magical devices she had installed in the backyard and was consulting them in a never-ending rotation. I took Sophie's hand, and the two of us stepped back into the past.

"Be quick," Sophie said, already beginning her dance.

"I will," I said, and jogged to the front yard and then next door to ring the bell.

Tompkins recognized me at once and brought me into the parlor. He didn't argue when I insisted on not taking off my cloak. A maid had just brought in a tray of tea when Coco emerged from a little door in the corner of the room.

"I'm surprised your father hasn't boarded those up," I said.

"I would never let him," she said. But her voice, her very posture, was devoid of most of its usual exuberance. She sat in the chair beside mine and poured out the tea.

"How are you doing?" I asked.

"Well enough," she said, putting two cubes of sugar into her tea and stirring it with a spoon. "Better than my mother." She held out the sugar bowl to me, but I shook my head. Everything about her, from the proper way she was crossing her ankles and holding her teacup to the softness of her voice, was completely unlike the Coco I knew and loved. I hoped it was just an effect of the grief that would fade with time.

But I was afraid it wasn't. Maybe that girl was gone now.

"You left very suddenly that night," Coco said between sips of tea.

"Yes, I'm sorry. Your mother was still very upset, and I was afraid seeing me might make it harder for her. That's why we didn't stop to say good-bye."

"You're probably right about that," she said. "She heard some of the things that Charlotte was saying in the library. About Edward and you. Blaming you."

"Do *you* blame me?" I asked.

Coco looked down at her tea. "No. I've thought about it a lot. I know you and Edward were friends. But the day you met Edward, he was already pining for my sister. I don't believe Charlotte was right about his feelings. And I certainly don't believe you pushed your way into anything."

"Thank you," I said. "I was hoping you felt that way."

"Yes," Coco said, still looking down at her tea. "I've been thinking about Charlotte too. All of the times since we were little, little kids when she would do something that bothered me. Sometimes even scared me. And how I never really thought it meant anything. And what might have happened if I had taken her more seriously and said something to someone."

"Coco, this is absolutely not your fault," I said. "Her own family didn't notice anything was wrong. And you two were never exactly friends."

"Maybe she could have used a friend, though," she said.

"Coco," I said, but then stopped. How could I explain what I had seen?

Coco looked up at me expectantly, but I couldn't find the words. She shifted in her chair. "I know Charlotte wasn't wrong about everything," she said.

"What do you mean?" I asked.

"I know you three can do things normal people can't do," she said.

"Maybe you don't call yourselves witches, but you're definitely something."

"How do you know this?"

"Brianna and Sophie weren't very careful about what they were saying when they were trying to use that key to find Charlotte," Coco said. "I was with them, but I think they kept forgetting I was there. And Otto knows too, doesn't he?"

"He does," I said.

"I thought so." She looked down at her hands, fingers twisting together. "I don't actually remember what happened up on that balcony. I mean, I don't remember it any differently. I don't know for sure if it was a stranger who came up the steps or if it was Charlotte who knocked me down and threw Ivy over the rail."

"You sounded very sure when you told the police," I said.

"Brianna and Sophie said what they were doing would lead us to the killer. At first I thought they were crazy. They couldn't agree which way to go and I couldn't even see what they were seeing. But then all at once they were both dead sure, and they ran straight to where Charlotte was. And the look in Charlotte's eyes..." She stopped fidgeting and set her hands neatly on her lap. "I know she's the one. And you three solved the case using, I guess, magic."

"Did you want to ask me any questions about it?"

Coco took a deep breath. "No. I think it's probably better if I don't."

"That might be true," I said. "But there is one thing I have to tell you."

"All right."

"It's difficult to explain, so I'll just tell you that I can look at a person and see things about them. How they connect with the rest of the world mainly, but also other things. When I looked at Charlotte, she had a darkness in her. All through her. There was very little of her left that wasn't darkness. She must have been like that for quite some time, perhaps since birth. I promise you, there was nothing you could have done to save her."

"I see," Coco said. She picked up her tea again. "She's in an asylum now. Her mother can't really afford it, but Thomas' father insisted on paying for her care. I think he hopes if she gets well again, that it will help him understand why all this happened. But I don't think it will, will it? I don't think she can get well."

"I hope she can," I said. "But I don't know if she will."

Coco sighed raggedly.

"Have you been back to school yet?" I asked.

"No, it's still winter break," she said. "But my friends have been stopping by."

"That's good," I said. "You're going to need your friends."

"Yes," she said. "Edward has stopped by as well. I think that's awkward for my parents. My mother won't come down when he is here. My father always tries to speak with him, but he never knows quite what to say. But everyday Edward has been here. We just sit together, and I suppose we're both thinking of Ivy, but somehow that's a comfort."

I picked up my cup and drained the last of my tea. I longed to ask at what hour he usually called, but at the same time, I really didn't want to know. I couldn't do anything with that knowledge anyway. I needed to get back to my own time.

"You have to go now, don't you?" Coco asked, too perceptive by half.

"I'm afraid I do," I said, standing up and straightening out the folds of the cloak.

"And you won't be coming back," she guessed.

"I would like to," I said. "I would love to come back and see you again, and I hope if I did that I would find you healthy and happy. But I'm not sure if that will ever be possible." I gave her a little smile. "As much as I'm a witch, I'm not a very good witch. And it's become dangerous for me to be here."

"You're not going to say good-bye to Edward?" she asked, genuinely distressed.

"I'm afraid not," I said. "Perhaps you can say good-bye for me?"

"No, I won't," she said stubbornly. "You're just going to have to get better at being a witch so you can come back and do it yourself. Only then, it won't be good-bye at all."

"Thank you, Coco," I said. "I'll always feel stronger knowing you're in my corner."

She got up from her chair to hug me tight then disappeared back through her little door before Tompkins came to show me out.

I interrupted Sophie's dance and the two of us cross the time bridge back to our own January.

"Did you see him?" Brianna asked.

I shook my head then took a wavering breath until the urge to cry passed.

"And how was Coco?" Sophie asked.

"Coco is as to be expected," I said. "But she did make me promise to learn how to be a better witch. So I suppose I should get started on that."

"Back to the library, then?" Brianna asked with a smile.

"Back to the library."

Sophie and Brianna ran up to the steps to the back door, but I turned to look one more time at the time bridge. It wasn't safe now, but I knew someday I would be crossing it again. My life was as much in 1928 as it was in 2019.

And I was, after all, a time witch. That was my calling. It couldn't be ignored.

COMING SOON!

The Witches Three will return in Charm His Pants Off, out on July 16, 2019 and available for preorder now!

A surprise ring at the doorbell on Valentine's Day confirms Amanda Clarke's suspicions. Her friend Sophie DuBois left someone behind when she came to Miss Zenobia Weekes' Charm School for Exceptional Young Ladies.

But the happy reunion grinds to a confusing halt when he asks about Sophie's quest to find her mother. And Amanda remembers she too came in search of answers about her own mother. Brianna Collins as well.

All of them forgetting their mothers the moment they showed up at the charm school? Someone, somehow, put a spell on them. But why?

Unless they find the witch who stole their memories, they may never know.

"Charm His Pants Off", Book 5 in the Witches Three Cozy Mystery series. If you're a fan of Amanda M. Lee, N.M. Howell, or Amy Boyles, this mélange of magic and murder mystery is sure to charm you.

COMING SOON!

Charm His Pants Off, Book 5 in the Witches Three Cozy Mystery Series!

ABOUT THE AUTHOR

Cate Martin is a mystery writer who lives in Minneapolis, Minnesota.

ALSO BY CATE MARTIN

The Witches Three Cozy Mystery Series

Charm School

Work Like a Charm

Third Time is a Charm

Old World Charm

Charm his Pants Off (coming July 16, 2019)

Charm Offensive (coming September 2019)

Made in the USA
Monee, IL
06 December 2019